Haven

H.L. Swan

Dedicated to my Grandma, who I can say with absolute certainty is the best Grandma in the world. If you disagree, you are wrong. (I love you. Please skip past the dirty parts.)

Also, for the worlds okayest brother. I know you won't read this, so someone tell him. Love you Bubba.

"Love doesn't have to be perfect. It just needs to be true."

- Beauty and the Beast

ONE

The wind gently rustled through the trees, creating a calming breeze that hugged my body. Dozens of starlings chirped with the rising sun as I tip-toed through the rolling, lush fields and deeply inhaled the crisp mountain air. Butterflies danced freely in my stomach. I could always tell when he was near, and the anticipation of seeing him never grew old.

"Alexander," I said softly, turning towards the sound of his familiar baritone, my crimson hair falling against my shoulders.

He stepped further into the clearing, making his way past two large moss-covered rocks. His crooked grin made my heart sing while his dark hair danced above his brow line from the breeze.

Moments later, the sun peeked above the towering trees surrounding us, creating a golden glow that cascaded through our meadow. Sunlight danced across my face, warming my cheeks.

My sundress floated with me as I made my way to his open arms. Picking up his pace, he advanced further onto the field to close the gap between our bodies.

My heart bounced in my chest. His face was a mixture of pure bliss with equal parts agony as he grew near.

But we both knew that we couldn't get too close.

My eyes trailed across the field, watching as the darkness seeped through the breaks in the trees. Falling like fog and slowly blanketing the soft blades at my feet.

I took in a deep breath, knowing what was coming next.

Without warning, it swarmed. Swirling around us like a wave, crashing through the brilliant blue sky to devour everything in its path. It wasn't the kind of night sky one would see at midnight with twinkling stars, but instead more of the kind of a light switch being flipped off in a damp, terrifying, endless basement created.

The wind howled violently around us, and urgency set in when I ran towards the other half of my soul. The longing in my heart took over my fear of the darkness that was now obstructing the perfect view I had of him only moments ago.

"Alexander!" I screamed into the void, but the howling winds of the forest muffled my cries. My hair whipped around my face as tears began to fall down my cheeks.

I could feel my heart sinking in my chest. As hard as we tried, as fast as we could pull, the darkness would always rear up and separate us.

I could no longer see him. Not his glorious, ocean eyes nor the tiny freckles that dotted his nose. I'd always caught glimpses of his features when the monstrous lightning bolts crashed into the space between us time and time again. Briefly, Alexander's face would show in the fleeting brightness.

Sadness was the best word to describe him in those moments.

My heart shattered in two at the sound of a deep, vicious growl emanating inside his broad chest. But no matter how dark and somber the forest looked, I always felt safe with him near. A familiar pain rose in my chest and crept into my heart. The longing I've felt so many times as the other half of my soul would appear, never within my reach.

A loud buzzing began to drown out the intensifying storm sweeping over the trees.

Beep.

Beep.

Beep.

Then, I woke up.

The buzzing of my alarm clock crashes through the still, morning silence. My palm smashes against the snooze button so I can return to sleepy serenity for a moment before the inevitable flood of emotion courses through me.

I can still smell the crisp mountain air while I nestle into my bed for comfort, still feel the sting of violent wind against my face.

It's always the same outcome in these dreams no matter what I do.

I've dreamt of the same man, in the same fields, since I was sixteen years old. But the ending is a never-ending loop, with us being torn from each other. Forever apart, forever untouching.

My tired eyes pan angrily to the clock on my nightstand, but they widen when I see the time. 'Shit!" I curse under my breath, ripping off my heavy comforter and hurrying to Mia's room. I exhale as I knock on her door, letting myself come back to reality from my all-too-vividly-real dreams.

When she doesn't answer, I turn to shouting. "Mia, be downstairs in five minutes, or you'll be late!"

"I don't care if I'm late. I don't want to go." Her attitude rubs off on me, causing my eyes to roll. Of course, she's worried about her recital. I'm not sure if it's the fear of performing in front of the judges, or the possibility of rejection that makes her so snappy.

"Five minutes, Mia, or we're having broccoli for

dinner." Not wanting to argue with my little sister, I return to my room.

Unfortunately, I don't have time for a shower, even if I do desperately need one. Sighing, I walk over to the bathroom and dash through a robotic routine of wash, rinse, repeat.

A thud sounds when my feet hit the cold tile floor outside the shower. I quickly run a brush through my now-soaking crimson hair before throwing on my scrubs.

Next, I head downstairs to find a smiling Mia waiting at the table. I internally cheer. The broccoli threat always does the trick.

"You look cute." I tell her, fixing her blonde ponytail.

She clutches her notebook, blushing. "Thanks, Ari."

I pour her some cereal before grabbing a bowl for myself.

"Damnit!" I hiss.

Mia's finger shoots up. "Bad word." She spouts, an annoying habit of hers.

"Sorry." I grumble, quietly sliding my empty bowl back into the cupboard so Mia doesn't realize I'm skipping breakfast again. "Did you do your homework last night?" I ask, shooting her a glance.

She nods before saying, "Mhmm." I don't miss the little giggles that keep escaping her.

"What is it?" I ask, raising a brow.

She tilts her head and studies me. "Who is Alexander?" Hearing his name, my blood runs cold.

Carefully I say, "Why do you ask?"

Her mouth curls into a mischievous grin. "You keep saying his name in your sleep," She begins laughing outright.

"Oh, Alexander." Mia coos in mocking tones. "I love you, Alexander." She flips her ponytail around.

"It was just a dream," I frown, playfully swatting her arm. "Now shush or you'll wake Dad up." Our gazes dart to the living room couch in unison, both of us silently pleading to remain invisible.

While I'm distracted, she slides her bowl in front of me.

"I'm not hungry." I lie.

With a shrug, she holds the bowl firmly in place. "I get breakfast at school." she states, her nose crinkling in a serious manner.

I devour the food before ushering her out. "Now, get to the car, you're going to make me late." I sigh and she dashes outside. Before leaving, I pry an empty vodka bottle from my father's drunken hands and chuck the contents in the trash. That's the third time this week I've found him this way, and the sight makes me sick to my stomach.

I wish I could say he wasn't always like this, but I'd be lying. Luckily, it's not something we've had to deal with for long. It's also not something I plan on living with for more time than absolutely necessary.

One day, I'll get out of here, but I can't leave my little sister behind. I'm old enough to adopt her, but I can't fully support her on my own right now. Not that I get much help here, but a roof over our heads is crucial.

My dreams – no matter how haunting they are – are infinitely better than my life. But Mia? I can't leave her behind, and although I've graduated college and have started a good job, I'm drowning in student loans and bills.

But I know with every ounce of determination in me that we will make our great escape soon.

TWO

I pull my latex gloves down tighter on my hands, steadying my breath to get into work mode.

"Okay, Timmy. You've got to promise me you'll stop trying to fly." I say as sternly as I can muster.

Timmy sighs, holding up his casted arm and offering a pathetic expression. "But Johnny said he flies off trees all the time."

His mother, Kendall, has had enough of the antics. "Johnny is a liar and a bad influence! Son, humans can't fly." She snaps.

"Well he did. He told me so." Timmy replies, his eight-year-old imagination getting the better of him.

Kendall looks to me with pleading eyes. "I'm so sorry, Ms. Castelle. He's got quite the imagination."

"That's okay. My little sister is his age, so I get it." I feign a smile, having a hard time relating considering Mia is a stickler for good behavior most of the time.

Timmy rolls his head back. "He's not lying." he cries. I admire the wild imagination and sincere curiosity of a child. One believing in fairytales without a second thought, even as his mother and nurse tell him otherwise.

I look to Kendall, handing her his paperwork. "His arm will have to be in the cast for six weeks. But for his cuts, I suggest applying flowering yarrow paste to them daily."

Dr. Devers walks in, shaking his head at me. "When are you going to start recommending real medicine to my patients, Ms. Castelle?"

Kendall smiles at the doctor. "That's quite alright. I prefer it, as it's much safer than chemicals."

Dr. Devers huffs before moving to have a word with Timmy.

I lean in to whisper with Kendall, knowing exactly how the Doctor feels about my preferred methods of healing the body. "Here's instructions on how to use the flowering yarrow as well as my turmeric paste for keeping infections away. Just don't tell him," I nod my head in the direction of Devers and wink.

I've only recently graduated nursing school, and while I've only been here for a month, I've seen little Timmy three times. I'm thankful Mia's never been the adventurous type, although I would prefer her to have more friends her age. She's so wrapped up in her music and our lives that she never really takes the time to be a kid.

When they leave, Dr. Devers gives me yet another lecture about medicine, one to which I nod my head and feign agreement. When Mom was sick, I saw what her medicines did to her body, and while she may have never recovered from her illness with any form of medicine, I feel like she would have been more comfortable.

My goal in life is to one day open my own clinic so I can help others. While I fully believe in all forms of medicine, I also believe in natural remedies, so I hope I'll be able to pursue my dreams one day.

Mia walks in, chucking her bookbag on the table and giving me a sour face.

"You better not be making broccoli for dinner." she says hotly, squinting her eyes at me. I'm thankful for the after-school program that keeps children until six before the bus brings them home so that parents can work, or in our case… sisters.

I stifle a laugh, having just gotten home and desperately unprepared for dinner. "I'm not! Let me see …" I rummage the pantry, cursing myself for not swinging by the store on the way home. Luckily, a frozen pizza is hidden deep within the freezer. "Pizza night?" I ask, raising a brow.

"Yay! That's perfect." She squeals, pulling out her binder and getting started on homework.

I preheat the oven and toss the pizza in, pulling out papers of my own to budget our monthly bills. While I'm in a good position with work now, we're still struggling. With the harrowing mixture of Mom's medical debt, bills, and student loans, I have no room for error.

Frank's house is paid for, and that is the only contribution my father gives. He's too drunk to find work, and I've got to keep food on the table along with lights for us to see.

By this rate, I'll be able to financially support myself and Mia in a mere ten years. With all of the expenses, I'll have a grand total of thirty dollars for us to live off of for the next two weeks.

"I'm so sick of this." I mutter to myself. Mia turns her face up from her homework in inquiry and I luckily remember her recital. "How was your rehearsal?" I deflect.

She beams. "It was wonderful. I got a solo!"

I do a little dance in my seat. "That's amazing! I told you that you would! Congrats," I smile, my heart full knowing that she has something positive going on in her life.

"Thanks, Ari." She looks away and bites her lip. I can tell she wants to say something.

I put down my papers and set my elbows on the

table. "What is it?"

She inhales. "I know you do a lot, and I'm really sorry to ask ..." She trails off, nervous, before clearing her throat. "The Orchestra director said I need new strings to play the lead."

"That's fine." I assure her. I'll find a way. I always do.

She grins. "Thanks, Ari." Then, her nose wiggles. "Oh no,"

"What?" I ask, but the moment that all-too-familiar burnt stench seeps into my nose, I know. "Shit!"

"Bad word!" Mia yells.

I huff, grabbing an oven mitt and tossing the burnt pizza onto the stovetop. "Mia, I'm exhausted. I've worked ten hours straight, give me a break, please." Why is it sometimes she can be so understanding, and other times so annoyingly immature?

"But I'm hungry," she whines.

I look around. "I am too. I'll fix something else, okay?" I suggest, praying for a break.

Mia shakes her head. "I wish Mom were here. She wouldn't burn the stupid pizza!" Her words cut like a knife, and I attempt to shake them off. Before I can find words to say back, Mia rushes to her room in tears.

"I wish she were here too." I whisper, my thoughts rolling back to how lucky we were. The loss doesn't lessen, it doesn't leave.

With the nauseating stench of burnt pizza wafting through the kitchen, I light a lavender scented candle and place it on the counter. The doorbell rings, and I lazily walk to it, knowing it's going to be my father. He'll probably be stumbling in drunk from the bar, as usual.

I let out an annoyed sigh when I see who is standing on the other side. This visitor was definitely unexpected, and not in the least welcome.

A shrill voice sounds from behind the door, "Hey," It's Dan, my ex.

I don't even bother fixing my hair as he walks in, uninvited.

"You haven't returned my calls." he says, giving me an accusatory glare. He throws his elbows on the bar top while I discard the burnt pizza.

"That's because we broke up, remember?" I tell him with a frosty glare.

He flashes an award-winning smile, but I don't fall for it. "Ari, you know how this works. You get mad and break up with me, but you always come back."

I shake my head, stifling a laugh. "No, Dan. You cheated on me, and you always show up thinking I'll take you back." Aside from his wandering eyes, the truth is that Dan has never been enough for me. That may sound harsh, but he doesn't get me. Not in the way that ...

The thought is useless, and my imagination needs to wind down.

He throws his head back, changing the subject. "You could come live with me. Get out of this dump."

"What about Mia?" I ask for the hell of it, already knowing what his answer will be. This is the same conversation we've had dozens of times.

He shrugs. "She's not your problem."

I cut him off with a wave of my hand, "First off, she's not a 'problem,' and secondly, we are not together."

Dan crosses his arms, standing up. "Why are you always so stubborn? Just live a little." he chides.

At the perfect timing, dear old Dad stumbles through the door. "Who the fuck are you?" he slurs, pointing a crooked finger at my ex.

"Arianna's boyfriend," Dan replies curtly, seeming unfazed by the fact that he's met my dad numerous times and the conversation always flows like this.

Dad grabs a beer from the fridge and leans against the counter for support, knocking off my freshly-lit lavender candle in the process. Glass shards spread everywhere, and hot wax splashes across the floor.

"Clean this shit up." he spits at me.

For once, I throw the towel in, literally. "No, get it yourself." I'm emotionally and physically exhausted, can't I have a break? Dealing with him is just another chore. An annoying chore.

Dan sends me a pleading look. "Arianna, do as your father asks. Just clean it." He shrugs, acting as though he has a say in any of this.

"This is exactly why we're not together." I tell him, still confused as to why he's even here. We were never serious; our relationship never held any depth.

"What?" He raises his brow, confusion settling on his face.

I walk towards him and he steps back each time.

"You have no backbone. You can't even stick up for me to my own drunken father? I don't want to see you again!" He continues to walk backward as I walk forward. I slam the door in his face when his feet land on the front porch before turning to rush upstairs, now fed up with everyone and everything.

I collapse onto my bed, shoving my comforter over my body while tears flow onto my pillow.

I try to imagine a different life for myself, one that I'll never experience fully.

It's a childish dream that I have, one to live with Alexander in his magical, dreamy land. I assume that he has a small cottage next to a river. We would have three children who would grow up to be happy. That's all one can wish for. We would live a simple life and on a summer day, Alexander would fish for us and I would hang up laundry to dry in the fresh breeze. These are things I think of to help me fall asleep. To let me escape, if only for a brief moment.

THREE

Tonight, for the first time since I was sixteen years old, my dream was different. It held a new location and a bright, inviting feeling. Instead of being in the typical wide clearing, the scene was more intimate. My bare feet gently landed on smooth, cool stones.

An elaborate garden decorated with roses, herbs, and endless flowers that I've never seen before spread out before my eyes. Ivy crept around and hugged tightly to the alabaster statues dotting the area. It was glorious and smelled of a sweet spring morning.

I went to sleep crying, and dried tears still lingered on my cheeks, but a smile crept on my face when I saw Alexander waiting for me by a sparkling fountain in the middle of the garden. He plucked a single rose from a nearby bush and held it out, as if I could ever get close enough to accept his gift.

All that separated us was a short cobblestone path. When he grinned, I walked closer. I advanced my steps, hoping that my legs would move faster than the force that would inevitably separate us.

"Hello, my love." His voice was smooth like honey, yet deep and inviting. I had grown accustomed to hearing his gritted tone, the one he used when in pain and torn away from me.

Although our meetings were always met with terror, we've had small fragments of meaningful conversation throughout the years. Learning little blips of each other's lives as we rushed to meet in frantic sprints.

This was different; his tone was thick with need and, for once, in no hurry.

My anxious eyes traveled around. While I wanted my gaze to stay on him, I couldn't control the fear that pooled in my stomach.

"What's happening? Why are we here?" I whispered, afraid that if I spoke too loud, the inevitable darkness would arise. I couldn't help that I kept looking away, waiting for the endless storm.

A crooked grin spread across his face, the usual gruff tremble in his tone vanishing. "Arianna's Garden?" Alexander questioned, flashing a stupidly arrogant smile that melted me whole. "I made this space for you so that when you come home you can spend your time somewhere as beautiful as you."

The words caught in my throat. "Home?" I finally asked, creeping towards him slowly, feeling the cool crunch of the soft pebbles beneath my toes. I wanted to dive into him but stopped short a few steps away. Something anxious and unsure clenched inside my chest.

"Come to me." His voice was confident, sure, and stern.

I shook my head, pouting slightly. "I don't want to leave just yet," I said softly, never having been this close for this long.

He extended his hand. "Trust me, Ari."

And I did. I followed the sound of his silky voice and took those few steps.

Our chests nearly touched, and my gaze had to crawl up his long body until finally, I saw his sharp face. The blue sky above seemed to perfectly match his eyes.

Alexander stayed still as a statue while I slowly looked left, then right, all too afraid that even the slightest movement would cause a reaction I couldn't bear to handle.

A cry flew from my lips as I dove into him, inhaling his heady scent for the first time. His strong arms invited me, protected me, entrapped me to him.

"Rain." I inhaled. "You smell like rain and pepper." I told him. He caressed my face with a small smile.

"Pepper?" He chuckled, his fingers running through my hair. He let out a sigh of relief when he pulled me closer, holding our bodies together so tightly that I relished in the feeling of security. "You're even more beautiful in person."

He appeared to struggle to pull back, seeming to fight within himself to either hold me against him or to get a closer view of my face for the first time. I was thankful when he decided to gaze down at me, his head dipping and his dark hair a tousled mess hanging above his brow.

I admired the way the sun glistened against Alexander's face, showcasing sharp curves and a dimpled grin. With his hard edges, he resembled the hand carved statues that lined the cobblestone pathway of the garden. He was pure perfection.

I flushed crimson when his ocean eyes scanned over my body. I'd never been this close to him before, and the simple feeling of his arms on my waist sent chills through my body.

Everything was quiet, serene. I looked to his broad shoulders and his unbuttoned white dress shirt. A tattoo peeked out from the collar, but I couldn't quite make out what it was.

I took in an invigorating breath, trying not to pass out from the closeness of our bodies. "How can you be so calm?" I asked, but I could feel the pounding beat of his heart whenever I laid my head on his chest. "I don't understand what's happening. Why aren't you getting pulled away from me?"

He grinned, and his crooked smile nearly made me swoon. "We can be together now, Arianna."

"How?" I was eager now, not paying attention to the fact that I was dreaming anymore. I enjoyed this strange exchange with him whenever I went to sleep. The only constant in my life has always been him. The moments I've spent with him in my dreams have been better than any reality I've ever faced.

I wanted him to take his time, but I equally wanted to know everything he did. Most importantly, why his confidence had shifted and how he felt comfortable enough to take such a longing moment as to twirl my crimson hair between his fingers.

"The darkness no longer encircles us; the gates are open for you. Now, just find me." His eyes bore into mine when he placed a freshly cut rose stem in my hand. Dewy droplets trickled onto my skin from the smooth petals.

His hands lingered on my wrist, and his striking white teeth gently bit against his bottom lip. All I could think of was how exquisite it would feel if his lips touched mine. Could we? No. It was much too risky.

I looked around the garden in an attempt to find something familiar, but I was at a loss knowing that we didn't have the things in my world that Alexander did in his.

It was a dream, a fantasy. So why did he feel so real?

"I don't know where you are. You're putting way too much confidence in me right now." I laughed the most nervous of laughs.

His carefree demeanor calmed the thundering of my heart. He put his left hand under my chin, gently pulling it up towards his face.

"I can only tell you one detail. It's up to you to find me from there." He said the words so simply, as if our lives didn't depend on finding each other. But his eyes told me the desperation behind his words. They were speaking to me what he couldn't dare say.

"What is it?" I whispered.

"Haven." Alexander replied.

My brow furrowed. "Heaven?"

He laughed, the melodic tone bouncing through the garden. "No, Haven. Your heart will lead the way." His eyes swept hungrily over my body, the low rumble of his voice catching me off guard.

I gulped. "Is that like in Connecticut or something?" I chuckled to hide the tears that now streamed down my cheeks. He felt so real, I could feel comforting warmth radiating from his body.

"What's a Connecticut?" He asked.

We both couldn't stop smiling, and my face began to feel sore from the happiness I felt coming to life inside me. It was the best kind of pain.

Instead of answering, I waved off his question.

"Where's Haven and where do I start?" I asked, allowing my dreams to entertain me just this once. I was aware enough to know that none of this was real, but still so swept up in the fairytale that I didn't care.

Alexander's ocean eyes bore into mine. "Find a waterfall." He held me upright when my head dramatically tilted back.

"You're joking right? Do you know how many there are?" I asked him, earning a shake of his head.

He took a moment to think, his fingertips gliding across the exposed skin of my neck. "You'll find it, Ari. You'll find me." He was so sure that I almost believe him.

I could feel myself beginning to wake, but I desperately wanted to stay. "No, Alexander!" I pleaded, desperate to live this fantasy just a few moments more. It couldn't just end like that.

But Alexander was a fighter. He would always slash through the darkness as a warrior would in battle just to get to me. This was different, though. This time, he let go of my hand, and looked at me with the most crucial, loving intent.

"I must go. I'm sorry, but we'll be together soon, my heart."

FOUR

M y eyes spring open, nearly blinding me from the harsh sunlight that bleeds in through my open curtains.

I jolt from the bed with a gasp, dried tears once again streaking my face. These dreams always feel so real that my heart physically hurts when I wake up without him. But this was obviously different.

I clench my fists, and my hands throb in pain. "Ouch!" I glance down, and my breathing ceases to a halt.

A single, thorny red rose lays on my palm where Alexander had placed it. The spiky thorns dig deeper into my skin as I hold on tighter, suffocating the rose.

"He's real." I mouth, stunned.

The years I've spent with Alexander have all been

real.

My skin is freshly pierced from the sharp thorns, and a small trickle of blood drips from my palm and onto the hardwood floor at my feet. I slowly place the delicate flower on my nightstand, peeling my eyes away from everything it tells me without saying anything at all.

Then, I frantically start packing my bags.

Grabbing random pieces of clothing and books, I shove them inside a duffel bag while murmuring to myself how impossible this all seems. But at the same time, I knew our truth all along.

He is, without a doubt, the realest thing I've ever had in my life, and I'm going to find him.

As my hopes rise with the sun, a tiny knock sounds on my door, and reality consumes me when I open it to find a sniffling Mia standing in front of me. Alexander may be real, but I can't just leave my life behind. I can't leave her behind. The thought of dragging her on something as silly as a dream is crazy, right?

But the rose.

The rose.

"I'm so sorry about last night." Mia cries, pulling me out of my thoughts. I bend down to comfort her. She wraps her slender arms around me, sobbing. I tilt her chin up,

"Mia, sisters fight, but that's okay. We're okay," I reassure her, but she shakes her head.

"You're all I have." Her tone is hoarse.

My heart shatters. "You're all I have too." *And Alexander.*

I wish Mom was here. She would know what to do, or at the very least, she would lock me away in a mental institution due to my crazy dreams.

"What do you want for breakfast? I can make pancakes. I hear your tummy grumbling!" I tickle her sides and she giggles before we head to the kitchen.

The broken remnants of my favorite candle are laid out on the floor, so I quickly pick up the shards of glass and discard them. I wish I had cleaned it last night so Mia didn't have to see it. But she can assume what it is, of course. Yet another one of Dad's screw ups.

I rummage through the pantry, my head swirling. "Where did I put the flour?"

Mia points over to the counter. "It's there. Don't burn these!" she jokes, her laughter traveling through the quiet house.

I smile, my mood elevated and depleted all at once. "I can't help it! I suck at cooking." I tell her. Taking a pinch of flour and flicking it in her direction, we're unable to contain our laughter and before long, we disturb the sleeping bear.

"Why are you being so fucking loud?" Frank's angered voice booms through the kitchen, his bloodshot eyes glaring us down when he emerges from the doorway.

Shit.

"I'm sorry Frank, I just ... it's Saturday and already eleven in the morning, I didn't think you'd still be asleep." I retort.

He stumbles, gesturing to the bag of flour. "You're going to need to pay extra rent if you keep eating all the food."

"You're joking right?" I ask in disbelief, as if he pays for groceries.

He shrugs. "I need money."

I scrunch my nose in disgust, trying to find the words to say but my rage boils over as I spot a new empty bottle of tequila by the couch.

"Mia needs new cello strings, and I don't have money to throw away on booze." Surprisingly, this is the most we've interacted in months. His eyes narrow into slits at my words, and he advances on me, the stench of alcohol weighing heavily in the air.

"You live under my roof, for free." he snarls.

"Free?" I choke. "Are you kidding me? You sit on your ass all day while I go to work and take care of Mia." I don't hide my disdain as I scream at him, fury guiding me. Even before I landed the job I have now, I was working all through nursing school at dead end jobs just to make ends meet.

"I don't want to hear your pity stories, Arianna. Just do your share." he yells back. The audacity he has astounds me.

"You aren't even aware of anything going on in our lives! Did you know that Mia made the lead in her school play?" I ask, raising my brows in frustration. It shouldn't surprise me when he shrugs, he's completely unfazed by the lack of involvement in our lives.

He grips the bag of flour and chunks it against the wall, resulting in a starchy snowfall surrounding us. I have trouble not choking on the thick air.

"I hate that your mother died. I would have never had to deal with you two screwing up my life." Frank bellows.

The crocodile tears that run-down Mia's cheeks break my heart. I take deep breaths to calm down, but it's not helping. She hops off the bar stool and marches towards us, her hands shaking.

"I hate you!" she screams at him. "We were having fun, and you always ruin it!"

"Don't disrespect me in my house. Go to your room!" he orders, getting in her face. I pull him away, trying to put a comfortable distance between him and my little sister.

A war is about to break out in our tiny kitchen, I can feel it. He peels himself from my grip, and the back of his palm violently collides with my cheek. I stagger back, dumbfounded.

"Are you serious?" I cry as the sting burns my

skin.

Mia stomps her foot, letting out a yelp. "Don't hurt my sister, you big jerk!" She punches him in the leg, with all of her might. Everything is happening too quickly for me to think but when he rears his hand back to her, I scream.

"If you touch her, you will never see us again." I threaten.

A greasy smile lights up his face. "Counting on it."

Whack.

Mia cries out, her arms extended in my direction. I sweep her in my arms and advance to him, without fear. "Get out! Get away from us." I seethe.

He stumbles away, grabbing a cold beer from the fridge on his way out the door, seemingly unfazed by the terror he just caused Mia. I set her down on the countertop. Taking one look at her, I make the decision for us. "We're going somewhere okay?"

"Where?" she cries, and the sound ignites a fire in me for us to escape all of this.

I think of how to explain my dreams and Alexander, but none of it will make sense to her. "Do you trust me?" I ask and she nods her head. "Then pack a bag. Not much, okay?"

She looks to me with teary eyes. "But where are we going?"

"To Alexander. He'll protect us."

She tilts her head. "From your dream?"

"He's real Mia and we're going to his ... town."

She listens intently, wiping her tears. "Can I bring my cello?"

A small laugh escapes me. "Yes, of course. One book bag and your cello. Don't get too—"

Before I can finish my sentence, she leaps off the counter and rushes up the stairs. I follow behind her with a hopeful smile.

In my room, I grab my half-packed bag and clasp my mother's necklace around my neck, for us to have something of hers.

I take a deep breath, walking out into the hall to meet a tear streaked, yet smiling Mia. "Ready?" I ask.

"Ready!" She chimes, looking hopeful.

We set out on an unknown route to a mysterious destination. But I'm not scared. I know with everything in me that this is my destiny.

FIVE

A m I losing my mind? One minute, I'm so sure, but the next, I let doubts seep in. Is this the responsible thing to do? Leave my job without notice and take Mia somewhere that may not even exist?

I twirl the very real rose stem between my fingers as we drive away from our house that never felt like home.

When Mom died, we had to move in with Frank. Mia was young. She still is, but her transition was easier than mine. Switching schools and towns didn't seem like a big deal for her; all she knew was that we missed Mom.

But now, she's a little older and doing well in her school. Even so, things certainly aren't better for her at home. It's not a safe environment, and we obviously needed to run far, far away from our sorry excuse of a father, but on a whim like this? I'm not sure what the right thing to do is.

At least she's safe. That's all I want for her.

"I'm excited to meet your boyfriend!" Mia says with a grin in the passenger seat. Her cheerful demeanor doesn't match the harsh truth of her cheek that's stained red from Frank's hand. I pat her head and give her a warming smile.

"I don't think he's my boyfriend ... but I am too." I reply, unable to hold back my grin. We've both been through so much, but we're strong and always bounce back.

She quirks her brow, studying me. "You've never met him?"

I shake my head, opening and closing my mouth as I try to decide what to say next. "Um, not yet."

"Oh," Mia nods her head. "That's confusing." Then, she shrugs, not thinking too much on it. "So, is he here in Rhode Island?"

I can't help the ridiculous laugh that escapes my lips. "Not exactly. Do you want to go camping?" I change the direction of our conversation.

"Camping?" She asks, confused.

I point to the backseat. "Yeah! I grabbed Dad's tent and everything."

"Why not a hotel?"

I feign shock. "What kind of adventure is staying in a hotel room?" I tease, "Continental breakfast? What a journey!" Mia laughs at my silly joke. "Maybe we could find chewed gum underneath a chair, too."

She scrunches her nose in disgust. "Ew! I want camping."

"Are you sure? We can totally get a hotel." I suggest. I have the money, but I won't find a waterfall in a Holiday Inn. I pulled all my savings out at the bank when we left, the money I had been raising to pay off Mom's debts while getting me and Mia away from Frank.

Plus, with the camping route if I have, in fact, completely lost my mind and we don't find Alexander, Mia will just think we were creating memories together.

She looks out the window, and I look forward, my mind reeling with anticipation. I researched a hundred waterfalls before we left, having no idea which one he wanted me to go to.

I decided to take his advice and follow my heart.

I just pray it leads me to him and not into the unknown, because I don't know how much more uncertainty my life can handle.

My fingers thrum on the steering wheel to the beat of the music from the car radio as my feet hover over the brake.

"Something feels right about this place."

Mia sits up, stretching. "How so?" She yawns.

"I'm not sure ... It's pretty?" I can't really explain to her the feeling that I know; it just is. She looks weary, but as we pull off the side of the road to a desolate area in the remote woods of North Carolina, she smiles.

"Ready to hike?" I ask, stepping onto overgrown grass and glancing into the wooded forest beside our Kia.

She nods her head, a wide smile taking over her face. I'm happy she's in good spirits after the horrible moment she experienced back at home. And that she's feeling well rested from sleeping the entire nine-hour drive.

As for me, I'm exhausted, but I have to give this a real try.

Mia quirks her brow when I grab her cello. "Why are you bringing that?"

I hoist our tent bag over my shoulder after putting on my backpack, my entire life stuffed into something so small. "Maybe I want you to play it!" I lie, knowing that if what Alexander says is true, we won't be coming back to this car.

"I can carry it." She offers, clutching onto her Tinker Bell backpack.

I shake my head. "No, it's too heavy. Just grab that bag for me," Unable to point, I nod my head towards the extra backpack in the trunk, the one holding our food.

We trek into the dense forest while I look to the map and mark a few trees with ribbon, just in case. As hopeful as I am, I also want us to be able to find our way out if all of this fails miserably.

"Ugh. Are we there yet?" Mia groans, dragging her feet against the damp earth.

I look around, quieting my mind to listen. Only hearing the chirping of birds, the steps of a far-off animal, gentle wind ... no water. I shake my head, and we continue further into the brush.

The sun on our backs sets faster than we can walk, and with the absence of the sound of rushing water around us, I begrudgingly decide it's time to set up camp. "Ready to stop?" I try to hide the disappointment in my tone.

She drops her belongings and lunges to a nearby tree. "I'll grab sticks! Mom taught us how to make a fire, remember?"

I nod, smiling at the memory. Mom was always connected with nature, taking us hiking on weekends when she wasn't at the clinic.

The only thing her and Frank had in common was nature. I'll never understand what such a strong and dedicated woman ever saw in a man like him. She was young and they didn't last, but she never remarried, and I'm not sure if her heart ever escaped him. It's a shame she never found someone to treasure her, because she certainly deserved it.

Luckily, since he didn't want to be a part of our lives, we never had to see him, and Mom wouldn't have allowed it. While she always harbored feelings for him, she had a lioness-like ferocity for protecting us.

Her worries when she lay on her death bed weren't of the unfair, shortened life that had been handed to her, or a fear of death. She didn't want us to fall into his hands, considering we had no other family. I assured her that we would make it work.

She became sick and then violently ill in only a short time. The cancer ate at her body until there was nothing left, and when she was gone, there was no place for us in this world.

A tear trickles down my cheek when I say my next words. "Yeah, she was pretty resourceful, huh?"

Mia nods, gathering small twigs and exploring around the campsite just a little further into the tree line. "Yup! And I'm going to make a fire just like her." She shouts back to me.

I set up our tent, giggling when she returns and attempts to make a spark from two rocks. I walk over and bend down, unable to tell her how she's doing it wrong. "Look, I see smoke!"

Her eyes narrow at the pile. "Where?"

I let out a quiet yelp and point behind her. "Oh my God! Is that a bear?" I shrill.

She turns quickly, and I flick a lighter on the dry leaves, igniting them. "Just kidding, no bear." I chuckle. She whirls around with her face scrunched, but her eyes widen when she sees the flames dancing on the ground.

"I did it!" she cheers.

We both sit in a daze, watching the red embers do an uncoordinated waltz above the flames. Finally, I grab Frank's camping utensils and some food I bought from a gas station I swung by while Mia was sleeping in the car.

"Smores!" Mia exclaims, snatching the bag of marshmallows from my hands.

I grab them back. "You have to eat your hot dog first." I tell her, but there's no conviction to anything I'm saying. All I can really think of is the absence of water, and in turn, Alexander.

"Are you okay, Ari?"

I nod, fixing my slumped posture. "Yeah, of course." I lie, trying to hide the desperate tremble in my voice. The pure devastation I feel as the night rolls on intensifies, and I realize my heart has only led me to the quiet woods of North Carolina.

Maybe my heart is broken. *Maybe I'm broken.*

Haven and Alexander are nowhere in sight.

Maybe I am losing my mind.

Long past midnight, Mia lays sound asleep beside me, unaware that we now have nowhere to go after we leave here tomorrow.

To not fall into a panic, I think of Alexander and the gentle baritone of his voice.

Small fragments of conversations dance through my weary mind. Those rare, blissful moments before the darkness would come to where we would get to know each other.

First, our names. Then, little bits about our families. But mostly, our untainted love for each other.

I think of him until I fall asleep because I know he'll be there.

He always is.

But the world is cruel, and it aches to destroy.

I'm twenty-four years old, and for the first time since I was sixteen, I didn't dream of Alexander.

SIX

I wake before Mia, unable to cope with the unfamiliar ache of Alexander's absence.

Seeing him in my dreams is routine for me. It's as simple as breathing air into my lungs, as normal and predictable as flowers blooming in spring. It's not a ritual I've ever considered could be stolen from me.

While it's always been a constant, I've never taken his presence for granted

Stepping out of the tent, the morning sun rushes through the breaks in the lush trees above. I inhale deeply, taking in the crisp smell of pine and the damp, earthy scent of the forest.

The sound of birds chirping calms me, the rushing sound of water makes me ... *Oh my God.*

I dash with frantic purpose towards the inviting

sound of flowing water, advancing on a mossy archway made of bending vines and twigs near our campsite. I know for a fact that this wasn't here yesterday.

Walking underneath the twisted canopy, a gasp escapes my parted lips while my eyes drink in the most magical waterfall, something out of this world, out of a fairytale.

It's so breathtakingly beautiful that all I can do is admire it for endless moments until I find myself being drawn to dive inside and swim to the bottom. To feel the crystal-clear waters against my skin.

It's magnificently large. The monstrous height demands all attention, making the typically large forest trees look like ants to a plane.

Gushing water cascades into a still, tranquil pool of sparkling waters.

"Mia!" I yell, not wanting to walk away. Too scared that it will disappear as fast as it appeared, but when she doesn't reply, I have no choice but to retreat.

Hesitantly, I turn and rush back to the campsite, waking Mia with a gentle, yet firm shake. "Ari, let me sleep," she begs like it's a Monday morning and I'm forcing her to go to school.

"Do you believe in magic?" I squeak, my enthusiastic tone much too bright for her to ignore.

Instantly, she perks up, her vivid imagination awakening her. "Yes..." she replies, looking at me with side eyes.

"What if I told you Alexander was magic?" I ask her, not paying attention to the weary, sleepy look she's giving me.

"Why are you messing with me?" Mia asks, sitting up and stretching.

I explain with great detail the magical waterfall and she looks at me uneasily, wanting to believe every word I speak but also being at an age where she's old enough to question the unexplainable.

I stand, pulling her with me. "Alexander lives in another world, Mia. I want us to go there. Do you want to do that, too?" I'm not sure what I'll do if she says no.

She smiles, shaking her head as I begin to grab our things. "What's there? Dragons?" Her tone is animated.

The vivid conversation draws me back to my childhood, reading fairytales with Mom. It may sound juvenile, but I've always believed in magic. That waterfall proves I wasn't wrong.

I send her a grin. "I'm not sure about dragons." I say, and she deflates. "But in my dreams—I mean from what Alexander told me, there's magic and fairies. Mushrooms as big as you! Pink waters that hold magical properties." I describe to her the things I've seen during my dreams, praying she says yes.

Because if she doesn't, we won't be going.

"It's up to you, Mia. It's a big decision, and I don't

know if we will be able to come back."

She still looks skeptical, and I don't blame her. "I want to see this waterfall first. I think you're messing with me."

I put a hand up, gliding it in front of me. "Just listen, Mia."

She freezes. "I hear water!" she stammers, her eyes as wide as saucers.

I grab our belongings, leaving the tent behind as we trek towards the alcove. I walk under first, turning around to catch her stunned expression when her eyes take in the gorgeous sight. "You can pick your jaw up off the floor." I joke.

"This wasn't here yesterday. I got our sticks right there!" Mia points to the water in shock.

I nod. "I know."

Her eyes roam up the enormous waterfall. "I've never seen anything like it." She speaks quietly, as if afraid to disturb the surrounding nature.

I clench my fists, excited and full of energy. "Do you want to go?"

"More than anything."

I can see the twinkle in her eye, but I have to be certain.

I lean down, trying to have as much of an adult conversation as I can with an eight-year-old. "Mia, if we go, I'm not sure if we can come back."

"I don't care. I have you and my cello. That's all I need," Her words hold so much power, I can tell she's as certain as I am.

"What about your school? Your play?" I ask.

She looks to me, shaking her head. "The kids weren't nice to me there." I frown at her honesty, never knowing. "I can play anywhere." She reaches out and touches the strings of her cello. "I mean it. I want to go, Ari."

Selfishly, I internally scream in delight.

"I just want to dive in." Mia mutters, her tone sounding mesmerized. "Why do I want to get in so badly?"

"I do too, Mia." I tell her, inching towards the water without trying.

Our bare toes dip into the sparkling liquid, and it's unusually warm considering the vast number of tall foliage around the forest that block out the sun. But then again, this wasn't here yesterday.

"Our stuff will get wet." She says as an afterthought, her bookbag already submerged on her back.

I nod. "I know ... but for some reason, I don't care." The water encases me like a warm blanket when I step in.

"I don't either." Mia replies. As if in a trance, we continue slowly walking in.

I fumble while holding our stuff, dropping my bag in, but when I grab it, a peculiar thing happens. "Look,

Mia!" I gasp, submerging it again to show her. She feels the bag underwater, eyes widening at it being perfectly untouched by the liquid.

"How is it dry?" She asks in an astonished tone. "Magic," She decides before I can answer her.

It's as if all her wildest dreams have come true, and before I can stop her, she plunges down. That same instinct to touch the bottom I had rushes through her. "Wait, Mia! You can't swim well!" I shriek, diving in after her.

I clench her massive cello against my body when I rush behind her beneath the waves. Everything that was heavy before feels weightless in this water as we both swim down.

Down.

Down.

Down until we reach the bottom, and my bare feet graze the softest sand beneath them. I try to open my eyes, but pure blackness surrounds me. I'm not scared of it, though; I can feel Mia holding my hand. Moments later, the water fades, and I'm left sitting on soft, spongy ground. My fingertips touch the padded area underneath me and when my eyes adjust, I look to them.

It's no longer daytime but pure night, and I'm sitting on a deep green moss that travels along the ground.

Upon looking up, a vibrant swirl of neon colors explodes before my eyes, illuminating from massive mushrooms that spurt out from the forest ground. Vibrant blues, sparkling greens, and luminescent whites shoot out from the mushrooms like the lively lights at a club. One thing I'm sure of is that this is definitely not the same forest we left. This is pure magic.

I search for Mia, finding her entranced. Her gaze is set on the luminous fungi that seems to flank a pathway. One after another springs to life, creating a blazing color and a distinct trail for us to follow.

"We're here, Mia." I announce in a quiet voice, not wanting to disturb the dark, yet inviting forest spread out before us.

"These mushrooms are just like you said, but they're way bigger!" she observes. I grab her wrist when she reaches out to touch one of the stalks, unsure if they're safe.

"I saw them from a distance I guess?" I question myself, never remembering them being this massive.

Mia lifts herself off the dirt. "In your dreams?"

As I stand, about to explain further, something captures my attention. From the corner of my vision I see fireflies emitting a powerful pink light down the pathway. They swirl up and down, left to right, in wild circles. I grab her hand and we begin to walk, knowing we need to follow them.

"I didn't want you to think I was crazy." I mutter.

"Too late, I already know you're crazy." she giggles

to herself.

I suck in a deep breath. "I've only seen Alexander in my dreams. I have every single night since I was sixteen." I leave out him not being there last night, worried why that may be. But now that I'm here, I know it must be where he told me to find him. He knew that I would.

Mia stares at me, but I can tell she believes my words. How else could I explain the things surrounding us if not for magic.

"You okay?" I ask her.

"It's just a little ...she looks around, stuttering. "Dark," She gulps.

I give her a reassuring smile, not feeling the least bit uneasy. "It's going to be okay. I wouldn't take you anywhere that would hurt you, I promise."

I gasp several times at the beauty of the dark forest. While I can't see beyond the pathway or mushrooms, I'm certain that it would be sensory overload for my brain.

"Look!" Mia exclaims while pointing, her voice echoing through the quiet forest.

In the distance, the spiraling pink trails reappear and swirl around a large tree ahead. But much to Mia's dismay, they disappear.

She frowns. "Do you think it could have been a fairy?"

I shake my head, trying to hold everything we own, along with her hand. "Not sure, everything is so unreal here. Let's just keep following the path."

And we do, until we reach a new archway made of creeping vines. That isn't what tells us that we've made it to the end of the trail, though. The sunshine that's beaming through does.

"It's daytime!" Mia announces, shocked.

I squint my eyes looking into the archway. It's like opening thick curtains into a dark room. "How weird is that?" I say, confusion setting in. When we left our world, it was day. Then, night. Now, day again. It's all too much to think about, and if Mia weren't here with me, I would have known I had lost my mind.

Right before we're about to rush towards the light, an unfamiliar voice alarms me. "Oh! I hear them. I hear them coming!" It's a woman, and I hear the whispers of others.

I grip Mia's hand a little tighter. "Mia, be very quiet." I tell her, unsure of my next move.

"Oh, Penelope! You're going to scare the poor lasses. Hush now!" Another unfamiliar female says, this one sounding more mature.

I don't move, I only speak. "Who's there?" I ask calmly, trying to hide the tremble in my tone.

"It's okay dear. Come out," The older woman's tone is comforting, but can one trust a voice?

I hesitate, looking towards my little sister.

I know nothing of this world. What if something

bad happens? As my eyes pan behind us, the mushrooms' radiant glow begins to fade, like they were only lit for us to find this clearing and nothing more.

Mia grips my shirt, tugging on it. "I think it's okay, Ari."

The pink, sparkly swirls appear again, guiding us closer to the mouth of the twisted vines.

With a brave face, I hold Mia tight as we step through the threshold. The bright sunlight irritates my eyes, and I rub them, trying to get a better view of what is in front of us.

A stunning landscape catches my attention, and a rolling, hilled countryside is the first thought that pops into my mind to describe the scene. The air smells of lavender and freshly-cut grass. Two women stand at the edge of the tree line, a man beside them. One woman is wearing a maid's outfit, her excited grin stretching from ear to ear. She has brown hair and rosy, plump cheeks.

The other woman is older, with pearly hair. Petite yet tall. She looks a little more serious, sporting an all-black attire with no fluff to it, but her smile is genuine.

"Oh, Arianna! We're so happy that you're here!" The younger woman squeals, clapping her hands together. She bends down and pinches Mia's cheeks, making them as equally pink as hers. "You too, little Mia!"

"How do you know my name?" Mia inquires, raising a brow.

"Alexander has told us everything about the two of you." The one with silver hair replies instead before throwing her palm to her forehead. "Where have my manners gone? I'm Ruby." Her smile lines are prominent, years of laughter streaking her face.

"And I'm Penelope," The younger one chimes. She seems like she wants to pull us both into a tight hug, but she restrains herself.

I extend my hand to them. "Hi, where are we?" I don't give our names, as they already know them, apparently. Everything feels like a dream, but I can feel everything around me in great detail. The way the soft grass feels beneath my bare feet, how the midday sun is warming my skin, the scents that surround me, and also, the scents that don't.

Rain and pepper. The sting of Alexander's absence alarms me, and I worry for him.

"Why, you're in Haven, of course!" Penelope beams.

She looks to the man who still hasn't spoken. "Pip, grab their things please."

I shake my head, already waving him off when he moves towards us. "It's alright, we can carry them."

Ruby scoffs. "No need. Pip is quite alright lugging them back."

He bows his head, a nervous smile on his lips. "Hello, Arianna."

"It's very nice to meet you, Pip." I say. "But—" Before I can detest, he's throwing our bags over his shoulder and gripping onto Chloe's cello. I feel bad that someone's helping us, but he seems eager to.

Ruby moves the silver hair from her eyes when the breeze catches us. "Alexander is going to be so thrilled you two made it okay."

"Alexander," I breathe his name into the crisp air. "Is he okay? Where is he?"

"He's quite taken with you." Ruby replies. "Come along, now. We must get going! Time is of the essence!" she chirps.

My heart squeals in delight, knowing not only is he okay, but that I'll get to meet him soon. My stomach flutters with anticipation; I've never felt this way before about anyone. "I can't wait!" I almost sing, my heart thundering inside my chest. These two ladies know my Alexander, and soon I will get to see him.

"You're every bit as lovely as he described!" Penelope smiles as we make our way north from the archway.

I blush from the compliment, thanking her. Mia huffs, seemingly jealous of all the attention she's not getting. She's always been that way, either wanting every ounce of the spotlight, or none at all. I imagine her dominating the stage in an orchestra one day, but I don't know if that's in her cards anymore.

"And you're as cute as a button. I have a granddaughter your age that will be thrilled to have a new friend, but we really must be going now." Ruby says, her tone light yet stern.

My intuition tells me I can trust them, and that's all I can really do now while we follow them over the spiraling fields of flowers and gorgeous rolling hills until buildings appear in the distance.

"We're almost home." Penelope announces, her hands gripping the bottom of her dress so she doesn't get it wet from the morning dew that blankets the ground.

The closer we get, the more everything comes into focus, and what we're walking towards is anything but a normal home.

"A castle!" Mia gasps, and she's not lying. The once smooth pillars stretch towards the sky like praying hands as they hold the ancient foundation in their palms. Centuries-old cracked marble wraps around the cylinders like a splattered web.

Every stacked stone on the castle walls are uneven and rugged, placed by hand with a thick clay paste to hold them together. It adds to the beauty, the sheer man-power it must have taken to build.

"Wow." I breathe, taking it all in. I can't even imagine what it must be like to live in something like that. I wonder where the village is and where Alexander lives. "I didn't know you had castles," I mutter, embarrassed by my lack of Haven knowledge.

Ruby gives us an inquisitive look. "Yes, of course. That's where we're going now. Are castles not normal where you come from? Where do your princes live?"

"Your princes?" I almost choke. "Why are we going to see Haven's prince? I'm in no shape to meet him!" The closer we get, the more I become aware of the bustling life surrounding the castle; horses with carriages ride along the streets and people flutter around the property.

A faint scent of smoked turkey legs wafts through the air, reminding me of the renaissance fair. But I'm happy to note the clothes on the townspeople aren't an example of medieval fashion, the garments aren't much different from my world.

But still, they're nicer than what I'm in now. I look to my bare feet and dirty clothes, shaking my head. I can't imagine the embarrassment I would give Alexander if I showed up to his prince's castle looking like this. "Can we go see Alexander first?" I plead.

Penelope places the back of her hand on my forehead. "Oh, she's exhausted from her journey. We must hurry and get her inside."

Mia pulls on my sleeve, her eyes filled with wonder. "Can I run through the halls like in the movies?"

"Mia, we're not going to the castle, we're going to see Alexander." I state, wondering why no one is listening to me. "It's packed, anyway!" I point to the mass of people at the bottom of the hill.

"Well, a royal wedding is underway." Penelope sings, gesturing to the masses of people.

I groan, pointing to myself. The women look over me, studying my appearance. "We can go through the back?" she suggests to Ruby.

Ruby nods, sending me a smile. "That would be best."

"Or we could go to the village? Let me get ready?" I suggest, trying to be polite, but I don't understand the rush to visit the prince.

"Arianna, you can't see Prince Alexander. Tradition states that you can't," Penelope pleads with me.

"Tradition? Prince Alexander?" I manage, eyes wide.

She laughs, and with a warm smile she captures my hands in hers. "In Haven, the night before any girl's wedding, she can't see the groom."

SEVEN

Penelope and Ruby usher us inside the castle, and I still can't fully grasp what was said outside. I'm getting married and I haven't even met him!

Not only that, Alexander is a prince. *A prince.*

The castle's extravagant architecture stuns me momentarily. Its intricate staircase, the marble flooring that seems to go on for miles with no end in sight, the crystal lights illuminating the ceiling.

We entered through a side door that was hugged by creeping ivy leaves. Hidden away from prying eyes, we slide through the empty halls quietly.

But even we can't escape everyone considering the sheer amount of metal-clad guards that dot the hallways, still as boulders when we pass.

Mia extends her hand, moving to poke one of their

hands, and I profusely apologize. The knight lifts his shield and tilts his head down to us, kind green eyes winking. The gesture almost manages to calm my nerves. Almost.

Once we're down a more private hallway, I inhale, trying to collect myself. I can't deny the way it feels like home, although I've never been here before.

I stop a few yards down the hallway when my eyes catch on something.

"It's him." I whisper.

My breath hitches in my throat as my fingertips trace the gold frame of a painting. Alexander sits on a throne, looking regal in a royal uniform. The way they've captured him with the oil paint is exquisite, apart from a few things they've missed.

He's every bit as handsome as I remembered, but I can't help to wonder if I had the talent of an artist, would I be able to paint the curvature of his hard edges better with all of the years I'd dreamed of him?

In the painting, his dark hair isn't the usual tousled mess that I've grown accustomed to in my dreams, but instead is perfectly placed and styled. Damn him for looking so good in any situation.

His face looks slightly different, a little more rugged.

Ruby admires the painting with me. "Yes, dear. This was the day he joined The Shield."

When I raise my brow in inquiry, Ruby gestures to

the men that dot the halls, standing at attention.

"Do you see the guards around you? They're here to protect the castle, along with Haven. Alexander joined when he was eighteen. Against his mother's wishes, of course, but some men can't be stopped."

"So, he's like a soldier?" I wonder aloud, looking to the medals that are pinned to his jet-black suit.

She laughs. "Darling, he's more than a part of it. He's their leader."

Before I can wrap my head around that information, Mia is fake swooning beside me. "He's *so* handsome!" she squeals. "I can't wait to meet him!"

I turn to Ruby. Giant, glowing mushrooms, military pins, and strangers dance through my head, making my brain swirl.

It's overwhelming, and all I want is to see his face in person.

"I really appreciate everything, I do, but I've traveled worlds to meet him." My eyes pan to the portrait. "Can we please break tradition just this once?" I plead with her, unsure how I'm going to take another moment without him being in front of me.

With a polite shake of her head, she apologizes. "I'm sorry dear, if it were up to me, I would let you, but Alexander was adamant about this. He wanted everything to be perfect for you, and for the first time you see him to be as you're floating down the aisle."

"Don't you mean walking?" I question.

Penelope looks as though she's going to pass out. "Oh, dear Haven's no! Why would a bride walk to her groom? How odd!" she quakes.

I shake my head, not understanding. "I don't understand, I can't fly."

Penelope's pink cheeks bounce with her grin. "The fairies will carry you to him, that way no bad magic can get to you on your way."

"I want to see a fairy!" Mia exclaims, and almost immediately, she yawns.

"In due time, little one." Ruby replies to Mia, gesturing for us to follow her. As we walk down the endless corridor, Mia bounces ahead to walk with Penelope. I stay behind to match Ruby's slower pace.

She knows every nook and cranny of this castle, confident in her stride and at ease with the guards that stand watch. I wonder why there are so many, but it just adds another question to my already busy mind.

Ruby looks to me with kind eyes.

"Arianna, I know this must be extremely overwhelming for you, but I want you to know that you don't have to worry about a thing. Alexander made sure that your every wish was taken care of. We're all here for you."

"My only wish is to meet him," I mutter, feeling regret for speaking my mind at the sight of the short frown

I receive from Ruby. "I'm sorry I just—"

Ruby holds up her hand, sending me a warm smile, "No need to explain, dear. You will see him very soon, I promise. For now, let's get you two acquainted with your room and rested, shall we?"

"This place is huge!" Mia squeals, her running feet squeaking against the marble floors of our shared bedroom. It's prepared for guests, for us. A bottle of wine lays inside an ice bucket, while a silver platter dotted with colorful treats sits beside it.

Breathlessly, I walk past the endless vases of gorgeous flowers and through the open balcony doors onto a stone deck.

So very far from the ground, a spectacular view lays out before me. Trees of all different shapes and colors line the property to my right. To my left, a crystal-clear ocean shimmers against the setting sun. All of this on a backdrop of pink and purple sky.

As the sun disappears between two mountain peaks in the distance, I have to wonder if I'm dreaming.

"It all seems so unreal." I whisper to myself.

"Haven is a magical place full of amazing things!" Penelope's chipper tone frightens me. I didn't know she was right behind me.

I continue to look out. "Is there peace here?" I ask, something I long for Mia to experience. My eyes pan back when there's no answer to find both women looking to each other. Ruby nods to Penelope. "There is now."

I can't help myself, or my questions. "What is the Shield for?"

"To keep us safe." Penelope responds, then she backtracks. "We're always safe though, more so protected." She fidgets with her fingers. "With magic comes great responsibility!" She stammers. Her voice is high pitched, her finger floating up and down in front of her in a nervous manner.

Ruby shakes her head, ushering Penelope and Mia away from us. She closes the balcony doors to gain privacy with me. All that's surrounding us is still and silence. Her wrinkled fingers wrap around the railing. "Haven is safe because of the Warriors that protect it, Arianna. Because of men like Alexander" She tells me. "He wouldn't have brought you here if things weren't okay."

"So why all of the guards?" I ask. "I mean, if it's safe, surely there isn't a need for all of this."

Ruby sends me a warm grin. "Most of what you see now is for the wedding. Your wedding," She smirks.

"Penelope just seemed so nervous answering my question." I worry.

Ruby waves her hand in dismissal. "Because she's a worry wart," I raise my brow in inquiry. "A demonic wolf." She calmly replies.

"A ... a what?" I stammer.

Ruby laughs, "Something of legends, dear. Don't worry about all of that. None of us do." She gestures out to the nature spread before us. "There is a line of Warriors waiting to ward off any evil that dare come here."

"Are we safe to walk around?" I gulp, looking to the forest. Unable to believe that something so pristine, so beautiful, could ever harbor anything evil.

Ruby laughs, gently grasping my shoulder. "Of course! The knights shield Haven with a fierce protection. You're perfectly safe here." She dusts her hands. "Now, is there anything we can do for you?" I detect a smidge of secrecy to her answers, but I'll find out more soon.

I shake my head, trying to let the information sink in, but my mind won't stop bouncing around. "I ... I just don't understand why Alexander wouldn't want to see me. Do you think," I pause for a deep breath. "Do you think he truly wants me to be his wife?"

Penelope giggles behind us. Ruby rolls her eyes at the chipper maid listening in on our conversation. Her hands are bunched up under her chin, and her pink cheeks are raised. "Arianna, I've known our prince for a very long time. For as long as I can remember all he's done is talk about you."

Ruby smiles, stepping back inside. Mia sits on the bed, tinkering with a box. "It's true, the entire palace has been awaiting your arrival." Penelope chimes.

Their words help me to calm, slightly. "How was I

able to come here? Why now?"

Ruby places a gentle hand on my shoulder, "I'll let the prince explain all of those details to you. For now, make yourselves at home. This is your castle, after all." She reminds me.

"Thank you, Ruby." I beam, thankful to have a moment alone to collect my thoughts. "Thank you, Penelope."

"Oh, dear. Call me, Pen!" she groans.

I look to Mia, and her smile threatens to tear her face in half as the women exit the room. She immediately goes from a calm eight-year-old to a maniac, jumping on the bed, falling in a fit of giggles, all while clutching a peculiar box. "I can't believe it! I can't believe you're marrying a prince!" she exclaims.

"I know." I breathe, unable to believe it myself. I gesture for her to hand me the striking purple velvet box that sits in her hands.

I sit on the bed, and she plops down beside me, tilting her head while I carefully pull open the silk ribbon. "Do you want to marry him?" Mia asks.

"Yes, of course." I reply without hesitation. There's no doubt in my mind, but I can't help the sadness on my face from him being so close and me not being able to physically touch him.

"What's one more day?" Mia shrugs. Such wise words from my little sister makes me laugh. Especially since she's now running around the room acting like an airplane.

I ponder if they have airplanes here, or cars, for that matter. But I look down to the open box to find a cream-colored card sitting flush on top of a bag of herbs. The note is addressed to me.

Arianna,

I hope this gift finds you well. It's a calming tea blend, as I've heard you're fond of herbs.

From one healer to another, Willow.

What a sweet gesture. I wonder who this woman is. As I take in the room more, I notice cards tucked into the endless flowers and next to the treats. I search for a letter from Alexander, but don't find one.

Thankful for the warm welcome but missing such a huge piece, the only piece really of why I came here, I walk to the balcony to collect myself. "Did you look at the view?" I ask Mia, smiling when she dashes outside next to me.

"Purple trees!" she bellows.

I nod, taking in their vivid hues. "And the ocean literally sparkles," I notice. I hold tight to the railing and lean my head back, smiling to myself. "I can't believe Alexander is somewhere in this palace."

"You know..." A mischievous grin spreads on Mia's face. "You could go meet him tonight."

Dusk is falling rapidly, and the bustling castle has calmed. What once was the pitter patter of feet dashing through the halls has transformed to stillness.

We had dinner in our room. It was brought to us by the most exuberant chef named Gerardo. He wore a large white hat and laid the plates out for us, lifting the silver covers from the top and showcasing our meal like in a movie.

What I found peculiar was the man that was with him. He was around my age, and before we touched our plates, he sampled small pieces of our food, seemingly deeming them fit for us to eat. He didn't speak but instead bowed his head, and when he was done, he left.

I assured them it wasn't necessary, but they insisted.

Around twilight, Ruby didn't want to overwhelm us further. So, any curious workers left us be. I'm thankful people are happy we're here, though; I feel so welcome even having met only a few people.

I thought this experience would be different, with a calm life in a village, but with the wonderful people I've met so far and the calm feel of everything falling into place, it almost seems that this is how it was supposed to be all along.

I'm excited to meet everyone. Most importantly, my heart.

"Mia, can you play for me?" I ask, smiling when her face glows as she grips her cello.

We step out onto the balcony and she begins to play.

I get lost in song after song, thankful for her. There may be times where we fight—we are sisters after all—but I can't explain my gratitude for her trusting me. The only thing I would miss from my world is her, but I get the best of both worlds now, literally.

A million stars twinkle in the sky, telling me that it's time. We go back inside and have our tea that Willow made. It's sweet with a hint of chamomile and lavender. I tuck Mia in, but she shakes her head.

"Go find him! I'll stay here and pretend to be asleep, but you better tell me everything!" It's much past her bedtime, but how can I tell her no?

I'm so thankful she's taking all of this so well; she seems happy. I am too, but this is all a lot to take in.

I understand why an eight-year-old would be adjusting to a magical land and castles with princes and fairies, but I'm not eight, and while I respect their traditions, I've waited almost a decade to lay eyes on my Alexander in real life and until I see him, I won't feel fully comfortable.

"I'll be back." I announce with a smirk, checking my hair once more in the vanity mirror. I creep out of the bedroom wearing a sundress I brought from home.

The castle is immensely quiet compared to earlier, aside from the stop and go steps of guards every so often. My fingers trail on the red wallpaper lining the hallway, its intricate design inviting me to swirl my fingers in the grooves as I creep down the unfamiliar path.

A guard rounds a corner, and I dip into a small alcove. Once he passes, I continue. I have no idea where to look, but something tells me I need to go up.

So, so many stairs. Spiraling wrought iron dizzies my vision until finally, I make it to the top. Carefully, I tip toe down a never-ending corridor, my heart threatening to burst out of my chest.

At the end sits two heavy, cherrywood doors just begging to be opened.

Gently, I press my sweating palms to the smooth wooden surface. I'm surprised when they easily push open to reveal a dimly lit office.

No, not an office. More of a headquarters. Dimly lit, wide, and double the size of our already vast bedroom. A large circular table sits flush in the space, and heavy chairs surround it, but they're all empty.

A man stands with his back to me. Broad shoulders and tousled hair look out of the window, admiring the twinkling ocean as I did earlier. "Alexander," I breathe in a whisper, my heart dancing furiously.

He turns to me, and I take in his sharp features that are illuminated by the silver of moonlight. He opens his mouth as if to speak but stops himself as he glares at me. "What are you doing here?" He hisses, not moving towards me like I am to him.

"I'm ... I'm sorry?" I stammer, confused. My heart sinks at his stoic appearance and his uninterested voice.

Alexander nods once, pulling a hand from his crisp jacket pocket. "I'll see you tomorrow at our wedding." he states, his tone oozing annoyance. I must have mistaken his icy expression for a simple gaze when I walked in, and I can't control the lump that's taken residence in my throat.

"But ..." I step forward and he scoffs. "Don't you want to see me?" I whine, not caring if I sound desperate.

He looks back out the window for a moment. "We can do all of that later. Go back to your quarters with Mel."

"It's Mia." I remind him, tears trickling down my cheeks.

Alexander rolls his wrist, "Mia whatever." he snaps.

I'm dumbfounded, and the pit in my stomach is growing. "I've waited practically my entire life to meet you, and this is how you treat me?"

He looks to the clock with a rectangular faded outline around it above the fireplace, his expression not faltering from boredom. "Are you done now? I'm busy." he barks. Turning away from me, he grips the window seal and continues his leisurely business.

I don't hold back, my voice rising well above a

whisper. "You're nothing like the brilliant, loyal man of my dreams." I exclaim, trying to hold myself together despite my shaking words.

One deep, guttural laugh escapes him. Without turning, he responds in the most heart shattering tone. "Reality is a bitch, isn't it?"

EIGHT

I rush back to my room, wiping away any evidence of the heavy tears that won't stop falling down my cheeks. I desperately want to fly into the bedroom, slam the door, and lean my back against it while I collapse to the ground. But as I walk in, Mia is sitting patiently on the bed waiting to hear every little detail of my encounter with not-so-prince-charming.

"What's he like?" She swoons, eager to hear my response. "Is he as handsome as the painting?"

I plaster on a toothless grin. "He's so wonderful, Mia!" I lie, sitting down next to her on the bed.

Her green eyes twinkle, surely imagining a fairytale encounter "I'm so excited! I can't wait until I can meet him tomorrow." she sings.

"Oh, Mia!" I show her my teeth, attempting to pull

my face upward but unable to produce an actual smile. "He wants to meet you right now! Do you want to?"

She squeals in delight. "Of course!"

I think for a moment, my heart feels like a ton of bricks. "Okay, so he said to meet him at the forest. The one we came in at—I know it's dark out, but he's really excited to see you!" I attempt to hide the tremble in my tone.

"I'm not scared of the dark!" Who is she kidding? She's terrified of night. "Let's go see your Alexander!" She dashes off the bed.

From the moment I walked out of his office my sole focus was getting Mia out of here. We have to leave Haven, immediately.

"You have to be very quiet, okay?" I order her gently. Like thieves in the night, we tip-toe through the halls, dodging guards as we arrive near the side door we arrived through. Guards are stationed, unmoving. I laugh it off, telling her we have to sneak around for fun. We quietly make our way out through the back of the castle and into the familiar garden from the dream that changed everything.

The dream that told me I could come here, that Haven and Alexander would be my safe harbor in the storm that is my life. If only I would have known I was stepping into a nightmare, I would have never come.

Mia's fingertips glide on the flowers around her,

the night sky illuminating their petals. "This garden is amazing." she whispers.

"He made it for me," I choke, my eyes panning around the space. It looks different in the dark, eerily beautiful. "Be careful. Let the moonlight guide you." I tell her, pointing up to the twinkling sky. The last thing we need is for either of us to trip and make noise.

We walk along the forest line, an unfamiliar route, but I know where we need to go.

"Who lives there?" Mia gestures to a small cottage, one surrounded by large, barely glowing mushrooms. They remind me of Haven's version of a porch light.

"I'm not sure. It's beautiful isn't it?" I admire the tranquil feel of the cottage, wishing all of Haven was as perfect as it looked.

I finally breathe when I see the entrance to the forest. The opposite of earlier, sunlight beams through and hits the dark grass on our side.

"Look, Mia! He'll be right through there." I beam. We're almost safe, almost away from him.

But something doesn't feel right. That gut feeling that we're being watched alerts me. A twig snaps nearby and before I can grab Mia to throw her through the threshold, I hear Alexander's once familiar voice. Only now, his tone is hostile, evil. "Guards! Seize her!" he commands.

The shimmering sunshine that pours through the

archway gives me a striking view as I turn. Alexander stands firm, surrounded by three guards, knights really. One of them, covered in metal, lifts his helmet and addresses the prince. "Seize the princess?" he repeats, dumbfounded.

"Of course!" Alexander hisses. "She's trying to escape."

Three knights in total. The one with his shield lifted is tall and broad. One has a smaller frame, oddly shaped compared to the other two. The other two look between each other, their expressions shielded by their heavy helmets.

The one who has his off shakes his head. "Your Highness,"

Alexander's rage is growing with every moment that I'm not in his custody. "Follow my commands! Seize her. Don't let her out of your sight until our wedding." he insists, not allowing room for any opinions.

When they hesitate, Alexander advances on me, gripping my wrist and pulling me away from the light and into the darkness of the tree line. "You will obey me." he demands, his fingers trapping my wrist hard.

I cry out, trying to control the guttural sound that escapes me. "You're hurting me." I gulp, but the betrayal hurts worse than his grip.

"You wouldn't want me to harm your sister, right?" he threatens, his tone venomous.

My eyes plead with him. "Please, let us go! Please," I beg. Nothing is more important to me than her safety.

Alexander shakes his head. "No. Obey me, go back to the castle and stay put. Or else ..." His ominous threat lingers in the air. He releases my wrist with a violent flourish, and I shake the ache the grip from his fingers leaves and slowly retreat back to Mia.

Thankfully, she didn't hear our conversation or see his unforgivable actions. With every passing second, the bravery I felt to rush through the threshold with her becomes a memory. I can't risk anything happening to her, and it would make no difference if we did run. They would catch us.

I trap her hand in mine, defeated and without any guidance to tell me what to do, I hang my head down and walk back to the castle.

"Ari, what's happening? Why was Alexander yelling?" Mia whispers, sounding off questions I can't answer because I don't know the answers myself.

I can't speak properly; my voice is as shaken as me. "Are you okay?" I whisper, ignoring her other inquires.

She shakes her head. "No! He yelled at you." She trembles.

The further we walk away from the bright clearing, the more my anger flourishes. I look back towards my cruel prince, the moonlight casting a creepy shadow over his eyes. He can't make out the sneer that's on my face, or maybe he can.

As we pass by the treehouse, a girl around my age steps onto her porch looking somber. Her pink hair is still bright, even in the dark of night. I think about screaming for help, but who can I trust?

"Excuse me," One of the guards says quietly, while the other one, the smaller one, doesn't speak at all. "You'll have to be separated from your sister." He informs me.

"How dare you! Take us back to our room if you must, but I'll be damned if you rip me from Mia." I snap, looking around to find peace in the cruel prince trailing behind us and not in earshot.

The one who defied Prince Alexander steps forward, his helmet still pulled up. Now that he's closer, I recall his green eyes from earlier.

"You'll have to forgive Cedric's terrible manners, ma'am. You and your sister won't be separated." He extends his hand. "I'm Douglas." He smirks, laugh lines surrounding his kind eyes.

"Well thank you, Douglas." I shoot daggers at Cedric.

Another guard sounds off, "But the prince just said—"

Douglas cuts him off. "We can watch them from their room. She's our princess." He leaves no room for error; his kind green eyes close to threatening slits when another guard attempts to mutter a word to us.

I walk in a confused daze to our bedroom, feeling bile rise in my throat at the thought of marrying such a vile man. As soon as the door is closed, I break into tears and grab Mia.

Her little fist hits my chest once. "You promised we were safe! You said he was perfect!" She sobs in my arms, trembles taking over her body.

"I know Mia, I'm sorry. I'm so, so sorry." I play with her hair. "Here, go lay down and I'll sing to you, okay?"

Thankfully, she's exhausted and doesn't argue with me further. She climbs under the comforter and closes her eyes, tears flowing down her cheeks. I sing her a familiar song that Mom used to sing until she's fast asleep, then I jump into action.

For obvious reasons, I check the door, but it's locked. I dash next to the balcony, trying to imagine how we could possibly get down without falling to our death.

I refuse to give up, but tonight will have to be what it is. Surely, tomorrow during all of the hectic events of the sham wedding I can escape.

I lay my head down on the soft, silky pillow, drifting off to sleep quickly.

I wake inside of a dimly lit prison cell while wet hay lies beneath my body. The pungent stench of damp earth and mold invades my senses.

"Mia!" I scream for her, but she's nowhere in sight.

"Ari?" Alexander's voice is low, quiet, close.

I turn in terror, seeing him lying in the corner of the cell. His face is bloodied. Maybe I punched him when he took me here.

"Stay away from me!" I warn, scurrying away. I press my back deep into the rod iron bars that are holding me in like an animal.

He gives me a peculiar look. "My love, you're here." He gulps, dragging himself towards me, his breath ragged. Seeing him so helpless tears me apart, but he's not the man I fell in love with.

I begin to shake, crying out of fear. "What did you do with my sister?" I stammer.

Alexander's eyes widen. "You did make it to Haven." he says quietly. "Where is Mia? Isn't she with you?" His tone is coated in worry.

I scoff, shaking my head. "With me? I'm here with you! You bastard!" I bellow, my angered voice bouncing off the walls.

He sends me the smallest smile. "Ari, you're dreaming. I haven't been able to talk to you." With a grunt of pain, he pushes himself towards me.

"Don't come any closer!" I warn, holding my hands in a defensive position.

He places his hand on his chest. "I would never hurt you." he promises.

"Look!" I hold up my wrist, showcasing the bruises

he most certainly left on me.

His eyes become slits, a snarl taking over his voice. "That wasn't me." he growls.

"Oh, whatever. You're going to act like this was someone else? Like you have an evil twin?" I snap.

Alexander bows his head. "He's been gone for a decade. I thought he was dead."

"Wait." I pause. "You're serious?"

"You know I would never harm you; I love you. I can't believe you're actually here." Through his rugged, deep voice, his tone is light and comforting. The silky voice I've grown accustomed to, could it be?

I look away, my heart not able to take much more. "I'm scared to believe you." A tear trickles down my cheek.

"Ari, look at me." he pleads, and I do. "You love horses." he says next, but I'm sure many girls do. He continues when I don't respond. "When you were sixteen you ran away from home to find me." He grins at our shared memory that I had told him about in our dream. I didn't make it far; only a few miles until I returned home, but I never told anyone else.

His blue eyes hold so much sadness when he looks over my wrist. "And Mia, she loves the cello and hates broccoli." He laughs, but it's small.

His familiar scent lingers through the air. Even through thick mud and dried blood, I can still detect the faint scent of pepper and rain. I don't know how I didn't see it before, but it seems so obvious to me now.

It wasn't him.

In seconds, I dive into his broad chest. He coughs from the sudden impact and I draw away. "What's happening? Are you okay?" My tone has gone from a clipped bark to a worried tremble.

"He came for me." He mutters, attempting to control his dry cough.

"Your brother?" I ask.

His eyes are like slits. "Yes, Mason." He spits the name like venom, violent thoughts surely swirling through his mind.

I don't know what else to say besides the truth. "I'm so scared, Alexander."

He gently takes my wrist into his hand, kissing the bruises. I gasp at the whisper of his lips on my skin. "You have to come find me. Get me out of here so I can protect you." He sounds confident in me, as usual.

"Where are you?" I look around the space to find muddy floors clashing with muddy walls.

He keeps his tone calm. "Find Chloe. She'll help you."

Tears escape me, although I'm trying to stay strong. "I haven't met her; how will I know who she is?"

He coughs, but it's dry and fresh blood lays on his hand. "Trust me, you'll know when you see her. In the morning, ask Penelope where she is. If they ask, tell her I told you about her in your dreams before you came."

"Why before I came?" I question.

"He had guards with him. That's how they took me and now I don't know who I can trust. Two of his men beat me until I was unconscious and dragged me here. I was waiting for you by the entrance when they attacked." He bows his head. "You can't trust anyone."

Although I'm terrified, butterflies swirl through my stomach. "I'll find you." I promise him. My eyes pan over his bruised and bloodied body. "Are you going to be okay?"

Alexander laughs and it bounces off the thick walls "Yes, sweetheart. You don't have to worry about me. I just want to protect you, so I need you to find me." He shakes his head. "I just can't seem to figure out what Mason's plan is."

"I think I know." I say, and he looks to me in inquiry. "He's going to marry me tomorrow, Alexander."

His baby blue eyes swirl with anger and fury. "Over my dead body." He spits. I sob into his chest as he holds me tight.

My body trembles against him. "I'm so scared. He threatened to hurt Mia."

He squeezes me tighter, ignoring me when I try to stop him after hearing his painful grunts. "I won't let that happen; I promise you. Just find me tomorrow."

"I will." I swear, laying my head against his chest

to feel a sense of normalcy. Normally, I would fight to stay in my dreams, but now I need to wake. "I'm sorry I didn't realize it wasn't you." I say, guilt eating at me.

"Shh, don't worry about that. You came here for me. Everything was strange to you, and you clung to the only familiar thing you knew. I promise I was waiting, ready to show you your new home."

A small laugh escapes me, and despite the chaos surrounding us, he makes my heart feel light. "You mean my castle, prince."

Alexander's crooked grin melts me, but I can tell how much pain he is in from his eyes. He draws me in, brushing my crimson hair between his bloody fingers. "I didn't want to scare you away, princess."

"I'm waking up, I can feel it. I'll find you, Alexander. I promise."

"I know you will, and then I'm going to fucking kill Mason for laying his hands on you."

NINE

"I don't care! Our princess is allowed to roam wherever she damn well pleases. Now, step out of my way!" Ruby's angered roar travels through the closed bedroom door.

"Miss, please." A guard tries to reason with her, but she dares anyone to get in her way.

"I said move!" she demands. There's some light shuffling and then she bursts through the doors, shaking her head at Cedric.

I want to rush to her, to tell her everything, but Alexander didn't know who we could trust, besides Chloe. Something in my core tells me that Ruby and Penelope are good, but I don't want to risk anything.

"Good morning, Mia!" Penelope, who prefers to be called Pen, sings as she walks in, her already prominent cheeks shaded with blush.

"Hi," Mia replies, wiping her eyes. I had a very serious talk with her about lying and how it was necessary we do that today. No matter how hard it may be, we need to act like everything is okay.

"Good morning ladies." Ruby chimes. She glides to the heavy curtains and shoves them open, smothering the room in morning light. "I apologize for our ridiculous guards. Why in Haven did they have you two locked in here?" she inquires, her hands planted on her hips.

I look to Mia, shaking my head slightly. "We went for a walk last night and Alexander found us." I lie.

Pen shrieks. "Oh no! You could be cursed for centuries for seeing him." she croaks, her palm colliding with her forehead in a dramatic fashion that makes Mia giggle.

"Penelope, you know that's just an old tale. I bet he was so happy to meet you; I wish I could have seen his face." Ruby beams, her wrinkles bunching up into a happy grin.

Pen calms herself down with a few ragged breaths. "Yes, what a wonderful meeting it must have been!" She swoons. I look out to the balcony so they don't see the heartbreak on my face.

"It was ... breathtaking." I decide on the term.

Ruby gestures for both of us to get moving, "I'm sorry to drag you out of bed but we really must get going.

Your wedding day awaits you!" She seems more chipper than yesterday. Ruby is a straightforward woman, happy when she needs to be and serious at other times. I wish I could tell her what's going on, but I need to find Chloe.

"Mia, come with me to get ready!" Pen suggests with a melodic tone.

Before I can stop myself, I grunt. "No!" I yell, and when they give me an odd look I plaster on a smile. "I mean, it's my wedding day. I need my maid of honor."

Pen shakes her head. "Your maid of what? We're maids."

Their confusion is evident, so I tell a truth. "It's a tradition where I come from, we choose someone we love to help us get ready."

The women smile, nodding their heads, and I let out a breath of relief when they don't question it further. I'm eager to start this ridiculous sham of a wedding day and find Chloe.

I stretch my limbs, smiling from ear to ear. "So, let's get started! What's first?" I ask.

Pen claps her hands together, her infectious happiness almost trickling into me, and even I have to admit that I'm incredibly happy. Not because of the wedding, of course, but because soon I will be in Alexander's arms. "Breakfast, of course!" She grins. "Then, your dress!"

I've thought about my wedding dress a million

times. Daydreaming of marrying the only man I've ever really given my heart to, Alexander. But then, it was all a silly dream.

I'm going to choose the ugliest, most gaudy dress for Mason.

Gerardo arrives with great flourish like the night before, pushing a food trolley with his large chef's hat swaying with his heavy steps. "Good morning, beautiful ladies." he says, a tinge of accent to his tone. Then again, Alexander has an unusual accent to him, too. Servants trail behind him with more trays.

"Hello, Gerardo." Mia smiles. His happy, animated character brightens everyone's spirits. The wide array of delicious breakfast food doesn't hurt either.

The man from last night tips his head to us, taking a fork. "Ma'am," he speaks for the first time, cutting into a corner of the egg.

"Why do you do this?" I ask the man, unable to control my curious mind.

He looks to Gerardo, who gives him permission to tell. "I'm a food taster." he replies, his head still bowed.

"You can stand up straight." I tell him, uncomfortable with him feeling as though he needs to bow to me. "Now, why do you taste it? For quality?" I wonder.

"I'm tasting for poison." he replies with a matter of fact look.

Mia shrieks. "For what?" She shoves her plate

away.

"Poison." he repeats, with a smile.

I lay my napkin on my lap, looking to Mia. "It must be custom for them. Remember Mia, our worlds are different." I tell her, reminding her that the things we've grown accustomed to won't make sense here and that we need to respect other cultures and worlds. But still, I'm curious too. "May I ask, why you would ever take on this job?"

He looks down. "I was given this job. I was a thief ma'am." he tells me, bowing his head again.

I nod. "And you pay for your crimes three times a day, with the threat of death each time?" I ask, stunned but hiding my expression. He nods once. "And how long have you done so?" I prod. The room is silent as I speak to the man, no one saying a word. It's strange.

"One year." He frowns, and I assume the position opened up for him when the last taster died. I don't like that.

I let out a breath. "What's your name?"

He smiles, seemingly not used to kindness. "Artie, Ma'am."

"Thank you, Artie." I say, watching Gerardo's face light up. They seem to be close, and I wonder if he's thankful for me being cordial to him. Is it unusual to be nice to someone who has committed a crime in Haven? Surely, he's paid for those crimes over the past year.

The thought sticks with me through breakfast but floats away as Pen pulls me from the chair. "It's dress time!" she announces. In seconds, the room scatters, leaving me and Mia to put our shoes on.

I look to the floor length mirror, smoothing out my sundress and telling myself to stay strong. Grabbing Mia's hand, we head out, meeting Pen and Ruby in the hall.

Maids, butlers, knights, they all smile at us, waving and bowing as we exit the castle. "Would you like to ride in a carriage or walk?" Pen asks, about to raise her hand to one of the guards.

I inhale the crisp air, needing a little sunshine. "Walk, please." I'm still unsure of making decisions and people bowing to me. It all seems insane, and I don't know if it's the life I want or one that I can handle. All I know is that's Alexander's life, and I love him.

As we head away from the castle, walking on a cobblestone path, I breathe easier knowing that there's distance between us and Mason.

The pathway is leading us towards the vibrant mushroom forest again. The closer I get to the now dark archway that brought us here, the more my stomach flips. I wanted to escape last night, but now? I never want to leave; I want to save Alexander.

"Where are we going?" I ask, nearly tripping over the smooth stones beneath my feet.

Ruby grins. "To a clothing designer. You'll love

her,"

When we arrive, I recognize the small treehouse as being the little cottage we passed the night before. The same girl, around my age, rushes out with a frantic look on her face. "I'm freaking out!" Her fingers wrap through her pink hair, threatening to pull at it.

Pen places her hand over her chest. "Why?" Her eyes are wide in concern.

The girl rushes to us, nearly tackling me in a hug. "I've waited so long to meet you! Alexander has told me everything!" she cheers.

I breathe out in relief. "Chloe." I whisper in her hair. It smells of peonies.

"That's the name," She grins, placing her hand on my back. "Now, come inside. We have too much to discuss."

As we step inside her cottage, I admire the woodsy décor. Soft moss envelops a stone fireplace while twisting ivy gently creeps up the inside walls. It smells fresh, dewy. It's beautiful.

Chloe claps her tiny hands together. "First things first, I need your measurements." She looks from Ruby to Penelope and attempts to usher them outside. "I've got it from here, ladies. Make yourselves busy." she orders gently.

Ruby sighs, upset to not be in on the dress fitting. "Everything's taken care of. We can stay and help," she pleads.

Chloe huffs, and a trickle of her pink hair drops in her face. She shakes it off and grabs a long strip of measuring tape before wrapping the numbers along my waist, bringing her face close to my ear. I open my mouth to speak but she cuts me off with a whisper.

"They won't leave until you say they can go, Ari." Her words come out quick, quiet. "I'll help you find him, the real him." she murmurs.

A sound escapes my chest, and I cough to cover it. "I really need some morning tea." I touch my throat.

Ruby begins to rustle around the kitchen, her eyes roaming through the cabinets. "Where's your tea, Chloe?"

"Fresh out." she tells them, throwing her hands up. With a sigh, they both announce they'll be back soon.

Once they step out, I can't stand still. "How did you know?" I ask, pacing in her small living room.

"Last night, I saw them taking you away. Alexander would never do that. It has to be ..." She shakes her head, not wanting to believe it.

"Mason." I seethe. "Alexander told me last night."

She perks up. "Where is he?"

I recall the horrific sight from my dreams, and I burst into tears. Mia sits near, looking frightened. It's hard to pull yourself together when all you want to do is breakdown, but I have to have her near me. I can't risk her being out of my sight. "In my dreams, he was locked away," I sniffle. "He's hurt."

Chloe places a gentle hand on my shoulder, soothing me. "What did you see around you?"

"Hay, iron bars, and mud," I smell the fresh air of the greenery around us, the opposite of the stench from my dream. "And the most awful musty smell."

"Hm, that doesn't sound like the castle dungeon." With a flutter, she snaps her fingers. Pink glitter seems to swirl around her hand.

Mia gasps, rushing to us. "You're the fairy!" she shouts.

I smile at the realization. "From the forest, you lead us out of the mushroom path."

She nods. "Chloe Dust, at your service!" She flashes a bright smile, the pink swirl stops, and tissues float into her hand. "Here, wipe your tears. Everything will be okay." she assures me.

I was certain she would know where he is, but she doesn't, and the doubt that creeps inside of me nearly breaks my already crumbling resolve. "How can we find him?"

"You're connected to him, more than anything. I can feel his soul reaching for yours. May I?" Chloe extends her hand to my chest, hovering over my heart. I nod for her to continue whatever the hell this is.

Pink swirls wrap around my body. I look to Mia to make sure she isn't scared. She's not, of course, but instead is mesmerized by the glitter when it trickles and sparkles around me. Chloe's eyes shoot open, but she's not looking at anything in particular.

"He's with the trolls." she groans in disgust.

"Trolls?" I bury my face in my hands. So many things I don't know of this world, but so many are familiar from the story books I read as a child.

"I know it's overwhelming. Me and Alexander were both going to introduce you to things at a natural pace, but Mason screwed that up." She shakes her head.

"Is he close?" I ask, chest tight with worry.

To my dismay, she shakes her head. "It would take about a three-day journey."

All hope leaves my body. Soon, I'll be married to Mason, and god only knows what he will be capable of doing then.

"That's too long." I gulp.

Chloe whirls around, her bright grin much too happy for the news she just gave. "It would take three days if you weren't traveling with a fairy." She winks, instantly elevating my mood.

"I'm ready. Let's go now." I gently demand, trying my best to not be antsy.

"It isn't that easy." She frowns, and it looks odd on her small, cheerful face. "We still have the whole wedding extravaganza going on at the castle today." She begins to pace. "No, we have to be careful with this or Mason will have every guard looking for you. Word could travel to the trolls and they could move him or—" She pauses, looking over to Mia, not wanting to finish her sentence in front of my little sister.

I shake my head. "He's hurt. We have to get him soon."

With a nod, she grabs the tape. "We will prepare you for the day as usual. You both have to act as if nothing is wrong. Can you do that?"

We nod in unison. I know Mia is only eight, but she's used to keeping secrets; she's been through so much.

"Is there anyone you trust to watch her?" I ask.

Mia stomps her foot. "No! I'm coming with you to save Alexander." she snaps.

Chloe bends down to look at Mia. "Your sister is right. Trolls are dangerous, disgusting creatures." She turns her attention back to me. "My cousin will watch her."

"And we can trust her?" I ask, looking between them.

"Yes, I'm not sure who helped Mason take Alex, but I have an inkling suspicion that it isn't any of the women you've met. We will be careful, of course, but I've known them for hundreds of years."

My jaw drops. "Hundreds? I thought you were around my age."

"I'm twenty-seven." She grins. "Forever."

Her answer provokes more questions than I can

handle to ask. "So, what do we do now?"

She springs towards me, throwing the measuring tape out with a flourish. "It's time to design your wedding dress, my dear."

A knock sounds on the door, collecting our attention.

TEN

We later step outside of Chloe's treehouse to be met by a young girl with green hair. Her large eyes match those of Chloe's, full and brightly colored, always matching the vibrant hues of their hair. "Where is this Mia I keep hearing of?" She asks, her tone light and airy.

Mia's arms wrap around my waist. "You can trust her." I say quietly. I hate that she's so scared. It was never meant to be this way.

Chloe smiles down to her. "It's okay, Mia. Aurora will protect you."

Green sparkles flow from Aurora's hands. "What's your favorite treat?" She raises a brow playfully.

Mia doesn't look convinced. "Cupcakes," she mumbles. On a nearby tree stump, green swirls cover the grainy wood and when they disappear, an array of cupcakes is revealed.

"Oh!" Mia squeals, and Aurora smiles to me. From that moment, I know I can trust her. Alexander wouldn't have said Chloe's name if he didn't have faith in her, so I trust Chloe's word that Aurora will keep Mia safe. She takes Mia's hand as they go to examine the sweet treats.

Chloe ushers me inside. "Now, we need to get you ready."

My hands swipe the moss when we step in. "You have a beautiful home. I'm sorry I didn't say it before. I'm just so ... scared." I admit.

"I understand, and thank you! All of this will be over soon. We will save him when the time is right." She picks up her measuring tape, wrapping it around my body and nodding as she checks the numbers. "What do you want this dress to look like?"

"Terribly ugly." I decide.

Like a fairy godmother, she holds her finger up. "Your wish is my command." Fabric wraps itself around my body, cascading over me, and I can't help the surprised gasp that escapes my lips. I thought I would be picking out a dress from a rack, but in a magical world I should have known better.

"It's perfect!" I chuckle at my reflection. Giant ruffles dominate the dress while flakes of puke green confetti line the bottom. It's hideous. "I couldn't have dreamed of an uglier dress." I tell her with a mischievous grin.

Chloe places her hands on her hips and nods. "Thank you very much." Her sarcastic tone makes me laugh.

I'm getting anxious. "When will we know the right time to save him?"

Chloe looks unfazed, and I find myself jealous of her calm demeanor. "It will need to be in a moment where you could disappear without detection."

The doors burst open, making me scream. It's just Ruby and Pen rushing back inside. Their jaws simultaneously drop at the sight of me.

"Oh, dear Haven! What did you do to the poor girl?" Pen cries, covering her red lips with her hand.

Ruby hands me a cup of warm tea, and I smile at their reactions while taking a sip. "It's different." Ruby finally chimes in.

I squeal, clapping my hands. "It's the one!"

Pen grips the large ruffles that adorn the dress. "Are you sure? I mean it's so ... odd."

Chloe speaks up, trying not to laugh. "She loves it! It's her day, after all."

"Very true." Ruby agrees. "You look stunning, princess."

"Let's get this show on the road!" I announce.

The girls look at each other. "Show?" Pen shakes

her head. "You're not getting married on the road, sweet girl."

"Just an expression." I state, and we all burst into laughter. The only moment since I've arrived that I'm truly happy, knowing soon I'll be reunited with my one true love.

Chloe ruffles my wild hair, making Ruby scrunch her nose. We left it unbrushed and unruly on purpose. "Let's get you married, Ari." She grins.

Ruby looks around. "Where is little Mia?" She asks.

I feign a smile. "Chloe's cousin, Aurora is taking her to the castle now. She wanted to show her around." I lie, knowing Mia will be with Aurora until we come back for her.

I walk outside the cottage and to my delight, two carriages led by magnificent horses are attached to them. Pen and Ruby climb into the back carriage while Aurora joins me up front. What truly catches my eye is the brilliant, stark white horse that's attached by gold chains to the carriage.

Chloe climbs in first. "He puts on a good act." I whisper to her as I sit on the plush white seat, feeling the cool leather on my fingertips. This is a fairytale wedding, but it's too bad the beautiful white horse is bringing me to a monster.

Chloe can't suppress her joyous laughter. "This wasn't Mason's doing. Alexander had everything in order before your arrival. This was a gift from him." she says. I should have known that such a beautiful gift couldn't have been from someone as evil as Mason.

Butterflies swarm through my stomach at the idea of such a grand gesture, all for me.

"So, Mia is safe. What's the game plan for the rest?" I question, trying to flow with the moments as they pass. Not living day by day, but second by second.

"Yes, she'll be safe all day. Once we arrive, head to your room. Showing face at the castle is the most important part, but you'll have a brief time of winding down available. So, you go to your room, and I'll meet you there so we can escape."

"All of the people will be left waiting when I don't return." I let out a nervous chuckle. "I never thought I'd be a runaway bride."

Chloe's green eyes look to me sincerely. "You're just going to be running to your true groom, so there's no need to worry. Everyone will understand why, soon enough." she states. The closer we get to the castle, the harder I grip her hand.

Upon exiting the carriage, I walk up to the horse. Unable to go any further without touching its cloud-like fur. "Does she have a name?" I murmur, realizing with a mesmerizing gasp that this horse is in fact, a unicorn. An iridescent horn sits on her head, and I can hardly peel my eyes away from her beauty.

"No name yet." Chloe beams. "She's yours. Alexander wanted you to name her."

I gasp, wrapping my hands around the unicorn's neck for a soft hug. "Mine? She's so majestic! It's unbelievable." I look to the sweet, soft unicorn with its pink, iridescent horn. "I'm going to name you Cloud." I decide, stroking her mane.

"Neigh," Cloud replies, nudging her head carefully against me. Mia will absolutely love Cloud! Once this is all over, I'll show her to him.

After a moment, Chloe taps her heels. "Are you stalling?" she asks.

"Yes." I say, nervous about reentering the castle to face Mason.

She takes my arm. "Don't worry, we've got this."

Guards stand at the ready as I make my entrance into the castle walls, and I don't miss the odd looks some give at my choice in dress. The girls are waiting for me by the front door.

Ruby looks calm while Pen looks erratic. "We will head to the gardens momentarily. Alexander will be waiting for you there." Ruby tells me.

"I can't wait." The words burn my throat.

Ruby places her hand on the small of my back. "Shall we head to the women's quarters to wait?"

I look away from her. "I'm going to my room to grab a piece of jewelry first, if that's okay."

Pen, who is six shades of red and sweating nervously approaches me. "Need my help?" She fiddles with my dress, needing to have a task.

"No. Thank you, though. Why don't you go sit down and have some water. Are you okay?" I ask, concerned.

Ruby ushers Pen away. "She gets like this during big events. Grab a guard if you need anything," Ruby assures, disappearing from sight a few moments later.

I walk up the grand staircase, opening the door to my bedroom quietly. To my dismay, Mason is sitting on my bed.

His elbows are on his knees and his face is in his hands. He turns sharply to look at me, a hint of a smirk playing on his face. "You'll have to forgive me for last night." What is he getting at?

I do a little curtsy, but I don't know why. Nerves, I guess. "Of course. I was just overwhelmed. I'm sorry for running away," I reply, my heart in my throat.

He stands, making his way closer to me. "It was unforgivable what you did." Mason's finger brushes a loose strand of hair from my face. The gesture makes me want to punch him in the nose, but I refrain. "But it is our wedding day, so I will let it go unpunished."

Gee, thanks. Psycho. He finally looks at my dress, and he's unable to hide his disgust at my appearance. "Are you wearing that?" He sticks his nose in the air.

"Yes!" I twirl, showcasing the dress I had made just for him. "Do you love it?"

"It's …" He cups his chin, sucking in his cheeks. "Yes. You look … stunning." he lies.

From the corner of my eye, pink sparkles dance on the balcony. Chloe is here. "Well, you should be going. I'll meet you at the aisle."

"Yes," He grins, his greedy hands sliding up my ribs, nearly making me heave. "Soon you will be my bride." His gaze travels to the door, a sinister smile stretching up his face. "I'll see you shortly, Arianna."

Once he exits, tears stream down my face. I can only stay strong for so long. I burst through the balcony doors, frantically searching for Chloe. "Where did you go?" I whisper.

A little flutter flaps against my face, and my eyes widen at the sight of Chloe. She's two inches tall. "The look on his face when he saw that dress. Marvelous." She grins.

"I know." I chuckle, not only at that but at how extraordinarily tiny she is. She slaps her little knee, laughing from the memory of his horrified expression. "Please tell me I don't have to walk down the aisle." I groan.

"Why would you walk?" She scoffs.

I playfully roll my eyes. "Go, float, fly, just tell me I won't have to fake a ceremony."

"Oh, definitely not! Alexander would have my neck if I let Mason kiss you." Chloe shakes her shoulders, then taps her chin. "Come to think of it, when Alexander finds out Mason touched you just now, he's going to go to war."

I want to think she's joking but her facial expressions tell me she's deathly serious. "I don't want him to get hurt." I say, my brows furrowing.

She laughs, shaking her head. "Alexander is strong, powerful ... it's not him you should be worried about." she tells me.

"Who should I worry about then?" I ask, watching as she flutters down to sit in my palm.

"Anyone who stands in the way of him getting to you." She winks, flicking her wrist. I blink, and we're no longer on the balcony but in a forest.

"Woah." I almost trip on a winding stretch of wood as I attempt to catch my footing from the sudden change in scenery. My eyes trail along the smooth root to the rough trunk of a tree. They seem to stand like guardians over the delicate foliage.

She shrieks. "Sorry I forget you're not used to all of this!" Chloe is full sized again, making my head spin. "It's okay." I steady myself, inhaling the dewy scent around me. "Where to now?"

Chloe points west. "Right over that hill there's going to be a troll bridge." She scrunches her nose in disgust.

"Do fairies and trolls not get along?" I ask, noticing

her distaste in them from earlier.

She checks her nails, pursing her lips. "They're disgusting, uncivilized creatures." she spouts.

The statement worries me, and I look around the quiet forest trying to come up with a plan and failing. "How will we get him out?"

"With their weakness," She grins, her eyes roaming over me. "Mortals."

"Me?" I gulp, my stomach already tied in knots.

She nods. "Yes. Specifically, human flesh."

"What if they've already hurt Alexander?" I gasp, holding my hands against my mouth. She simply shakes her head. "How can you be sure they haven't?" I demand.

"Just am." She seems to want to say more but doesn't.

I cross my arms. "Chloe?" I strain, trying to solve the puzzle to her confusing answers. "How do you know? If they eat mortals, why haven't they eaten him?"

Chloe waves her hand dismissively. "That's a story for another time, but they don't want him. No, they're keeping him because someone gave them something they couldn't refuse. We just need to give them something better." she deflects, grabbing my hand.

"So, my life for his?" I think for a moment, coming to terms with such a decision. "Will you keep Mia safe when I'm gone?"

Chloe widens her eyes, a small gasp escaping her.

"Arianna, no! We're not going to sacrifice you, just trick them."

"Oh." I breathe out in relief.

She grins at me. "But it's good to know that without a second thought you would protect those you love, even at the cost of your life."

We set a plan in motion and I mull over every detail when we near the bridge, my heart pounding harder with every step. I gasp when I take in the sight of a large creature sitting by the stone walkway, guarding it.

"What is he doing?" I whisper to Chloe. My eyes feel like they're playing tricks on me.

"Trolls won't let you pass their bridge, but we don't need to. See how he's sitting there?" She points to him. "He's guarding a cave."

"Who goes there?" The thunderous roar of the troll's voice makes me quiver. His legs, the size of tree trunks and covered with winding hair, stretch out in front of him as he sits.

Chloe is unfazed when she steps out to get a better view. I follow meekly behind her, trying to avoid his terrifying gaze. "Hello, Krempan." She sneers.

He scoffs at the sight of her. "What business do you have here?" Every word he speaks has such a deep tone that it bounces off the moss-covered rocks and trees around and nearly vibrates the very forest floor under our feet.

"We want inside." she says with no hint of fear, and I have a new admiration for her cool demeanor.

He grabs his belly, laughing at her request. "No." he states flatly.

"I brought you something." Chloe sings, reaching her hand back to me. She ushers me out and I look to the bearded troll with terror in my eyes.

His eyes glide over me appreciatively. "A snack," He says. His large tongue darts out from his mouth and glides over his slimy lips. I refrain from hurling when we step closer until we're at the edge of his bridge. Mere feet away from the monstrous creature.

He inhales deeply, closing his eyes. "She won't do." he growls, turning his head away from us.

"Why not?" Chloe whines, growing irritated.

He looks to her. "She's undesirable. Rotten." He turns his wart filled nose up in disgust.

I shake my head. "Rotten?" I ask him, surprised by the lack of fear in my voice. Krempan gives me a singular nod and I turn to Chloe. "What does that mean?"

With her eyes creased, she shakes her head. "I'm not sure." She looks to Krempan. "What do you mean by that?"

He flicks his wrist, reminding me of a spoiled teenager. "I don't have time to waste explaining things to you. Leave." He orders.

Chloe inches forward, trying to reason with him.

"You have something of hers." she prods.

He scoffs. "What could I possibly have that would belong to that?"

"My soulmate!" I shout.

The ground shakes when the troll stands. He has to be at least twelve feet tall.

"It's okay. He won't hurt us." Chloe comforts me when she feels my body trembling.

His laugh is deep and stretches far beyond the area we're in. "Who says I won't?" he threatens.

"You have our prince, and we won't rest until he's back to us. Even if that means waging war on you, filthy beast." Chloe hisses.

Krempan's eyes widen in surprise. "Arianna." He mouths, looking at me with suspicion.

"How do you know my name?" I demand. My confident tone doesn't match how I feel.

"You're the girl he won't stop going on about. I didn't believe you were real. Thought he was going as crazy as a wild lynx," He rubs his stringy, brown beard. "The girl from his dreams is ... real?"

I'm staring at a twelve-foot troll, in a magical land, holding hands with a fairy. How could he not believe in dreams? "Will you please let him come back to me?" I ask, trying a different tactic. This time, it's softness.

"No!" He roars. "You have nothing I desire. Move along."

"We will give you anything you want." Chloe pleads, her strong resolve wavering.

He thinks over this for a moment, mulling over her solution. "Anything?" Krempan asks.

Frustrated, Chloe stomps her foot. "Yes! Anything, you impossible beast!"

This seems to irritate him. "Step away from my bridge! I've told you that I want nothing from you." He takes one menacing step towards us, the ground practically crumbling at his feet. I worry that when dirt falls, so will the cave and Alexander will be trapped inside forever.

"Ouch!" Krempan cries out, lifting his massive foot and limping back to his spot.

"Are you okay?" I can't help but ask, the caregiver in me taking center stage despite his monstrous appearance.

Chloe huffs, crossing her arms. "He's being a baby! Come on, we'll figure out another way."

Against my better judgment, I ignore Chloe. "Do you need help?" I ask the troll. He sits back down in his spot, and a thundering vibration rings through the forest again.

"No." he grunts, lying.

I tip toe closer, taking calculated steps. "I'm a nurse."

"I don't know what that means, and I don't care." he snaps, but I can see the pain in his face.

"You really are unreasonable!" I tell him, shaking my head. "It looks like there's something wrong with your foot." I push.

"I'm fine." he lies again.

I examine it from a distance, moving closer with every step. "It's bigger than the other one, painful from the looks of it. Why don't you let me help you?" I ask.

"I said I'm fine!" he roars.

Unafraid of him, I stomp my foot. "You're stubborn is what you are. Now, lay it out." His defiance reminds me of some of my patients. He hesitantly follows my request and lays his massive foot out in front of him so I can get a closer look.

"What is a nurse?" Krempan asks, his breathing heavy but his voice calmer than before.

"She's a healer," Chloe remarks, walking up beside me.

I examine his foot with a gulp, my nerves nearly getting the better of me. It looks like he's been stabbed by a large, sharp object. Infection has set in around the wound. "What happened?" I ask, and he tries to pull away.

With a frustrated huff, I won't let him move.

His foot is so large that I don't have to kneel or bend to examine it. I'm standing directly in front of it, and I doubt he can even see me from where he sits. He nearly cries out when my fingertips skim across the padding of his feet. "A few weeks ago, I got a splinter in my foot. I got it out, but it still hurts."

He gestures to a tree branch nearby, apparently his version of a splinter. "My foot won't heal." he whines and with a sigh, he stops trying to pull away. "My wife used her magic, but nothing helped."

I shake my head. "You don't need magic, Krempan. You need antibiotics." I tell him. He gives me an inquisitive, bushy brow and I realize he has no idea what that means. My holistic practices will do me good here. "Stay here. I'll be right back." I inform him, taking Chloe with me.

I trudge through the forest while Chloe follows close behind. "I need oregano," I murmur to myself, eyes searching high and low.

"We have that!" she cheers, excited that this transfer of services could mean getting Alexander back. "What else?"

"Wonderful! I need a ton of it. He's got a massive infection, and I am not trained to amputate." My eyes scan the bushes of berries. "Do you have any type of herbs for healing?"

Chloe zooms into the forest, returning moments later with handfuls of oregano and another unfamiliar herb. "What's this?" I ask, examining the bright blue color. It's a flower, but it's slightly glowing.

"Permidaisy! I don't know much about herbs, since magic is my trick. But our healer in town, Willow, uses this for tea whenever someone's sick."

Willow was the one who sent the wedding gift of herbs. I smile. "Perfect, can you make a cup of hot water? A tea drip maybe?"

Chloe smiles at my request, and pink swirls hover over her fingertips. "One cup, coming right up!"

I laugh remembering earlier when she sent Pen and Ruby back to the castle to get tea. It wasn't even necessary. Once she hands me what I need, I mash the ingredients together to create a thick paste.

"You came back." Krempan observes, his tone clipped yet relieved.

I nod. "Of course. Now, drink this while I apply the oregano paste to your foot." He seems hesitant at my request. "You can trust me." I assure him. No matter how mean someone is, I will always do my best to give them the best treatment I can.

Finally, he gives in and relaxes when I apply the paste. I make sure to coat the wound in the medicine and let Chloe use her magic to speed up the healing process.

Krempan wiggles his foot, and the slightest hint of a grin appears. "That's incredible. Thank you!" He marvels in the feeling of having his foot back to proper health.

I smile back. It feels good to help someone, and we've definitely won some brownie points with him. "So, can we get him now?" I ask, my tone beyond hopeful.

"No!" His thundering voice makes the ferns tremble. "What don't you understand of you have nothing that I want?" he bellows.

The pounding of large footsteps sounds off beside us and before I can yell at the troll, another one appears. "Krempan, you really are insufferable." He's taller and older, with white hair and a thick, long beard. He offers an apologetic expression. "Hello, young lady." His voice is loud, but much, much nicer than Krempan's.

I have the urge to extend my hand, but his is so much bigger than mine. "Hi, my name is Arianna. I'm just trying—"

He cuts me off with a wave of his hand. "No need to explain, dear. I heard everything. Krempan is being unreasonable." The troll sends him a serious look "She did you a deed, now let her in!"

"But Papa ..." Krempan groans. It's his dad. I have to crane my neck straight up to see their conversation.

"I said move, boy! And you better tell this young lady how thankful you are for her help, too." he demands.

Krempan huffs, stepping away from the entrance of the cave. "Thanks," he mutters, turning his back to us.

"What are you waiting for? Go in!" The elder gestures us inside, his sly smile alerting Chloe.

She grabs my hand and holds it tight. "I don't know about this. They're tricky creatures, Arianna."

He hears her whisper, and they both step away

from their bridge, showcasing they don't have ill intentions. "I'm going. Stay here, just in case."

I gulp as I step into the mouth of the dark cave, my fingertips gliding against the damp rock walls. "Alexander?" I call out, my voice echoing into the darkness, but there's no response.

The damp, shadowy corridor is a never-ending maze. It reminds me of an ant bed, having multiple directions you could go in with no way of knowing your true location, but dozens of opportunities to get lost. My only light takes the form of dimly lit lanterns placed far from one another across the stone walls surrounding me. I make a few turns, getting helplessly lost.

That is, until I come across familiar wet, thick mud with a pungent smell. I trudge through the cave with wide strides, the heft of my hideous wedding dress weighing me down.

"Alexander?" I repeat. His name bounces off the walls. From afar, I hear a clanking sound. The dark, rocky corridor is equipped with multiple cells, all of them empty.

A muffled groan fuels me to leap into action, and I run to the sound, desperately hoping it's him.

I nearly tumble down a steep set of stairs that seem to appear out of thin air. Taking a deep breath, I descend, sinking further into the cave and towards the familiar scent of damp earth that invades my senses, just like in my dream.

When I see his body hunched over, a pit of anguish flares in my stomach.

"Oh my God!" I cry out.

Alexander peers up through thick, dark lashes. He's bloody and bruised, but no one could mistake the shimmer of love that twirls in his eyes.

"Alexander." I breathe, relief flooding over me.

I lunge to the bars that hold him in. "Ari." His voice is even more lush in person, deep and inviting. My fingers grip the strong, horizontal metal but no matter how hard I pull, they won't budge.

I try to bend and twist until my bones feel like they're going to explode. "I can't get it open!" I stammer back, exhausting all my resources.

Alexander withers in his restraints while I gaze helplessly around the empty hall. "Why are you here alone?" he asks, voice hoarse as if he hasn't spoken in a long time. "Where's Chloe?"

A pink swirl sparkles in front of my face, lighting up the glimmer in my eyes. "Oh, dear Haven!" She squeals. Her small fairy frame sweeps through the iron bars, her hands clasping her cheeks. "Don't move! I'm going to untie you." Chloe tells him.

Alexander doesn't take his eyes off me, a protective glint in them. He has a look that says I need your body against mine, now. I shiver slightly at the thought.

Chloe floats around him, using her magic to

remove his restraints.

The heavy chains topple to the ground, announcing his freedom as they sink into the muddy floor. Alexander breathes my name, nearly tripping over himself to reach me. His hands slink through the rusted bars, encasing my face in his palms.

From opposite ends of the cage we watch each other, no words spoken. I dip my head into his embrace, a tear trickling down my cheek and landing on his wrist.

"Keep holding each other." Chloe orders and Alexander moves his hands to mine to grip me in a protective hold. She floats to our tangled hands, and I fear if I blink, I will lose him.

Desperate to hold on, I don't look away and I peel my eyes open, daring them to shut. His blue eyes capture mine, making everything around me fade until I see nothing but his face, his hands. I feel like I'm flying, like the world has become something bright and beautiful. Meanwhile, my heart is racing in my chest at being so close to him. I'm finally holding him after all this time.

He grins. It's crooked, and his white teeth shimmer against the sunlight that has suddenly blossomed inside the cell. Except, it's not a cell anymore, but a rolling hillside full of flowers. Without hesitation, his hands trap the small of my waist, pulling my body against his.

"I can't believe you're here." Alexander murmurs.

I bury my face into his neck and his hand gently

lays against my hair. I fit so perfectly into him.

"Guys, I really hate to break this up but you're very, very late to your wedding." Chloe tries to speak, but I barely hear her when Alexander cups my chin, my cheeks, my hair.

"Breathtaking." he says softly.

In the natural lighting I can see the full extent of his wounds. "You're hurt." I whisper nervously, my hands trembling.

Reaching into Chloe's backpack, I pull out the paste we made, laying it out thick on his open wounds. Chloe impatiently speeds the process with her magic. Everything heals apart from a crescent scar that sits underneath his left eye.

With a striking gaze, his eyes hover over my body before pulling me to him again. "I knew you would find me." Alexander chuckles into my hair.

"Always," I tell him. So lost in this moment, so utterly consumed by everything that he is, it takes Chloe yelling to break me from my trance.

"Okay, this is really adorable. It is, but Mason is still here, and we have got to go." she pleads, but she can't hide the smile on her face

"Right," Alexander's mood shifts as he steps away. I've only ever seen him clean shaven, but two days in prison has given him a deep shadow to compliment his sharp features. He cups his chin, thinking for a brief moment. "Take us to the castle. I need my guards to be ready." he orders Chloe.

His demeanor has become downright stoic, and he's ready for battle.

ELEVEN

"I'm so sorry that he hurt you. If I would have known he was alive ..." Alexander says, voice trailing off when he looks at me with pathetic eyes.

I stand with him, tucked away in the upstairs office where I first met Mason.

"It's not your fault. You thought he was dead, so how could you have known?" I ask, not wanting him to blame himself. I next gaze up at Chloe. "Is Mia safe? Away from here?"

"Yes!" she replies, her light tone and ambient attitude soothing my spirits. "Her and Aurora are inside Fairyville as we speak."

I don't ask questions since there would be way too many. Instead, I try to calm the anxiety forming in my chest at being separated from my sister for so long.

"Everyone is looking for you, Ari. The entire village and castle were at the wedding ceremony." Chloe remarks, having heard the gossip of the castle while we snuck in through the back earlier.

"What do we do?" I question, looking to Alexander for advice.

He glances at Chloe. "I need my men and my army."

"But there's someone you can't trust." she reminds him. Alexander paces the room, his stride mimicking what he is; a soldier, stiff and coordinated.

Finally, he speaks. "Where's my Father?"

From what little I know of his dad, they're close, especially since the passing of his mother.

"I'm not sure." Chloe looks around nervously, her fingers lingering on a chess board. "I haven't seen him since you went to wait for Ari."

"The night I was taken, then. Has anyone seen him?" Alexander demands, pure rage lining his eyes when she shakes her head no. The terrifying realization that his father is missing finally seems to dawn upon him.

I try to ease his worries with a comforting hand on his arm. "Would he really hurt his own father?"

"Mason is ruthless, controlled by rage and hungry for power." Alexander sneers, but he seems to cool slightly at my touch.

"Why did you think he was dead?" I prod,

attempting to understand this family dynamic and how it came to this.

Alexander shakes his head, not wanting to answer. "Chloe, find Douglas." he gently orders, but one could sense the irritation in his tone. He doesn't like this situation one bit, not being in control of what's going on around him.

"On it!" she chimes back, her light feet practically gliding her out of the office.

I put my hand on his chest next, feeling his racing heartbeat beneath my fingers. "We'll find him, Alexander." I promise, giving him a reassuring smile. "Who is Douglas? I met him, and he treated me well."

Alexander grins at the news. "My most trusted soldier." he replies.

Our conversation is natural, even in the midst of confusion and fear. He looks to me, a dimpled smirk now on his face since we're alone.

"I've thought about the moment we would first be together in my head so many times." Alexander says slowly, his voice like silk and full of desire. His hands graze my sides while his eyes search my own, as if hoping to find the same wanting in my gaze. I'm in desperate need for a distraction, and I can tell he is too.

"I have, too." I admit quietly as he moves closer, closing the gap between our bodies. My bottom hits the desk behind me while his fingers fist my crimson hair. He dips down, his lips a feather away from gracing mine. Nervous, I begin to ramble. "Nice desk," I breathe out, unsure what else to say.

"This desk has seen the wages of war, the plans to destroy and slaughter for battle." He sucks in a breath, inhaling my scent. "If we had time, it would have nothing on it besides you." The low hum in his voice sends heat to my core, igniting a fire inside me.

"We've got time." I gasp. I want to escape, if even for a moment, from all this madness.

"Ahem," A male cough sounds behind us. Simultaneously, we both look to the direction. Not realizing anyone else had entered the room, I blush crimson. "Alexander," Douglas says, nodding to us.

I've only ever seen him behind metal armor, but this time he's wearing a formal uniform. He's tall, with long dark hair pulled back into a slick ponytail. A silver streak on the left side of his hair catches my attention.

Chloe giggles in the corner, making a second intruder on our private moment.

Alexander takes his time lifting off me, as if to not rush the brush of his hand against mine as he walks away.

I watch with wonder when his demeanor shifts into something serious as he walks to greet Douglas. "Did you miss me?" Alexander asks. I can tell they're close when they hug, patting each other's backs with a rough slap.

"I knew from the moment Mason stalked back into

this castle that it wasn't you." Douglas admits, scratching his head. Alexander looks away, his clenched teeth revealing something I can't very well detect. Guilt seeps through me, and I feel that I should have known too. "No, darling." Douglas turns his attention to me. "He doesn't expect you to have known."

"Did I say that out loud?" I ask in shock, covering my mouth.

Alexander shakes his head, sighing at his friend. "Douglas can read minds."

Well that's just invasive. "Oh,"

Alexander untucks a braided cord from under his shirt collar. "Why has no one given her a stone?" he inquires.

"Sorry," Chloe feigns shock. "Must have slipped my mind when I realized you had been *kidnapped!*" Her sarcastic tone makes me laugh.

Alexander rolls his eyes at her, and in a quick movement he pulls the braided leather over my head. The cold stone hanging on the cord hits my skin, and his fingertips gently glide against the sensitive area of my neck.

I admire the emerald gem attached to it. "Malachite," I say, recognizing the stone almost immediately.

Douglas whistles low in approval. "You know your gems?" he asks, surprised.

"Of course!" I touch it with my fingertips in awe,

feeling the cool, smooth surface. "This is a protection gem."

Douglas nods his head, impressed. "It's also Haven's national stone." He announces, showcasing his. I look to Chloe to see that she has one on a bracelet. "Our ancestors enchanted all the Malachite centuries ago, enhancing its powers to protect us."

Alexander brushes my cheek with his fingertips. "But it will only protect your thoughts. You need to stick close to me for safety." His eyes bore into mine, and butterflies ignite and multiply inside me.

I look to his now bare neck. "Where's your protection?" I wonder aloud, raising a brow.

His eyes twinkle at my worry. "Don't fret about me. I have plenty of spares."

Douglas clears his throat, yet another person attempting to pull us out of our trance. "Sir, I'm sorry to interrupt, but your brother is trying to take your rightful place." he reminds us.

Alexander nods reluctantly, moving away from me so he can focus. "Very well. Do you know how he got back?"

Douglas shakes his head. "Not a clue. I've had my men searching for you in secret since the moment I saw him."

The subtle anger crosses Alexander's face again. "You knew, but you didn't warn Arianna?" he snaps, not hiding the contempt in his voice.

Douglas bows his head, offering me a solemn look. "I couldn't alert Mason. I'm sorry, Arianna."

I wish that he would have given me some clue, some form of truth to know that Alexander was in danger, but at the same time, I could never hold that against him. I wave it off with a smile. That's the least of our worries right now.

Alexander doesn't seem so easy to forgive.

"She is of the utmost importance. In any situation, we save the princess. Is that understood?" his tone oozes authority. Douglas nods and Alexander sends me a dimpled grin before focusing his attention back on the rescue mission at hand.

The men move to the heavy wooden table, mapping out a game plan. The room is still, and they don't speak for a long time while they're lost in thought. After a while, Alexander picks up what looks like a chess piece made of heavy stone. It slams on the table, and he slides it to another, identical piece. He's focused, drawn in by the fight he's mapping out in front of him.

Douglas sends him an idea, but he shakes his head. "No that won't do. We can't trust anyone until we do the enchanting." Alexander tells him.

"Yes, sir." Douglas replies. It's odd, hearing a man twenty years his senior calling Alexander sir, but he leads their army and is also Haven's prince.

I stand by, watching on in stiff silence. My mind hasn't stopped racing since I arrived here, and now my heart thunders in my chest if Alexander so much as breathes in my direction.

Chloe touches my shoulder, and I jump a little. "You okay?" she cocks her head, a concerned expression on her face.

"I'm fine." I lie quietly while Douglas and Alexander continue their hushed, strategy-filled discussion.

She playfully rolls her eyes at me. "You don't have to lie, you know. I'm your friend."

"Okay, full honesty?" I inhale a sharp breath when she nods, nervous that I'll offend her by my worries. Haven is all she's ever known, and everything here is normal to her. "I'm not okay, actually. I'm freaking out." I admit, running a hand through my crimson hair to release some of my stress. "What if Mason hurts him or his father? What if Mia is in danger when she gets back? There are so many questions I have but we can't slow down." I keep my tone low, not wanting to disturb Alexander and Douglas.

Chloe processes my rambling for a moment, taking the time to think of a reply. "This will all be over soon." she says finally, tone sure. "Alexander is great at what he does."

"And what would that be?" I inquire.

She rolls her wrist, seemingly not a worry on her mind. "Saving people, destroying evil." Chloe grins. "You know, the usual."

In that moment, Alexander peeks up through his dark lashes.

His blue eyes slice through me with hunger, and my butterflies return to their waltz inside my stomach. I trust him fully, wholeheartedly, and I hope he can't sense my fears, because they have nothing to do with my feelings for him.

"Do you want me to expel them?" Chloe asks curiously, her hands tangled together.

I peel my eyes from Alexander's sharp features, giving her a side-eyed glance. "Expel what?"

She lifts her pointer finger, and a little sparkle burst out. "The butterflies." Chloe deadpans, making me laugh nervously.

"I didn't know I said that out loud." I flush, trying to blanket my face with my hair.

"You didn't." She smirks.

I clasp my new gemstone, wondering how long this has protected Alexander's mind and feeling special that he gave it to me. "I thought no one could read my mind with this." My brows push together in confusion.

"I can't read your mind. I'm a fairy, not a wizard!" Chloe chuckles. "But that's not why I know they're in there. I can hear their wings flapping like crazy!"

"Oh," I mouth, gripping my stomach. "Well, that's okay." I respond. I'm so unaccustomed to the odd things they say here. "They aren't actual butterflies. It's just a saying."

If she says she can't hear my thoughts, can she tell from the blush on my cheeks, or can she actually hear them? No, that's madness! I'm going crazy.

With a slight giggle, Chloe trails her signature pink swirl over my body. To my surprise and slight horror, dozens of purple butterflies flutter out, their little wings carrying them around us and the room.

"Chloe!" I gasp, my cheeks reddening. But I can't help but admire their carefree dance.

"We've got a plan." Alexander announces, turning around and batting away the pretty butterflies with a confused expression while I ignore Chloe's laughs. We both stand like we've been caught doing something wrong.

"What is it?" I ask, not wanting to talk about this in the least.

Douglas steps closer. "We need him alive since we have questions for him." He swats one of the butterflies away.

Alexander sighs, a look of seething resentment taking residence in his normally calm eyes. "Yes, and I'll be the one to get answers from him. I need to know who brought him back to life," he hisses. "And how."

I hesitate, not wanting to overstep. "Maybe you were wrong. Maybe he was never dead in the first place."

"No, I know he was dead." Alexander looks away

from me, ashamed. "Because I killed him."

TWELVE

"You killed him?" I croak. I can't hide the surprise in my tone, and Douglas and Chloe exit into the hall to give us privacy.

"Yes." Alexander replies, his expression stoic and unreadable.

It's not my business, but I have to ask. "Why?"

He looks away, a distant memory seeming to form in his mind. "I wish I could explain, but we have to save my father." he reminds me. I perk up at his words, feeling guilty for having so many questions.

"I'm sorry it's not the right time. Where is he?" I question, bringing my hand to touch Alexander's stiff body. He calms at my touch, looking down at me with a nervous set to his jaw.

"We don't know. I'm going to have to torture

Mason until he tells me." He steps closer to me, his firm hands now gripping my chin. "I would never put you in harm, but Douglas thinks we could use you."

"I'll do anything." I say and mean it.

He shakes his head, immediately dismissing the idea. "Doesn't matter. I won't allow it. There has to be another way."

"Trust me. Please, let me help." I plead.

He cracks a dimpled grin, swaying when I pout my lip. "I can't risk anything happening to you. I only just got you back."

"You won't. What does he need me to do?"

"Oh, Alexander!" I sing song his name, but really, I'm trying to lure Mason out from whatever dark corner he's hiding in. I had to plead with Alexander multiple times before he finally agreed to follow Douglas's plan.

Still in my ridiculous gown, I hold it up while trudging through the damp grass near the castle. Chloe did a stakeout of the grounds and found him on the east side, surrounded by a couple men as they discussed something in a small huddle.

Standing near a separate gate, this one made of wood and surrounded by stacked stones, Mason steps out, seething. "Where were you?" he barks, advancing on me. I take in a deep breath to steel myself, knowing Alexander is hiding in the shadows waiting to protect me.

When he's directly in front of me, Mason shoves his finger in my face. "How dare you embarrass me!" His attempt at a thunderous roar reminds me of small dog yapping, and I have to hold back a laugh. I should have never feared Mason.

"Embarrass you?" I snort, placing my hand over my heart. Two of the guards exit the clearing to give us privacy.

"Yes, you stupid, stupid girl." His fingers squeeze tightly around my wrist. "Everyone was here to see us wed. Where were you?"

I use my free hand to flip my hair. "Oh, I was just hanging out with someone." My tone is carefree, buoyant.

"That stupid fairy?" he guesses with a sneer, and I clench my fists.

"Don't you dare speak of her that way!" I snap. His anger is focused so much on me that he doesn't notice who's behind him. "If you must know, I was spending time with Alexander." I calm my tone, nodding gracefully.

He stiffens. "Excuse me?"

"You know, the real Alexander." I smirk. Mason's eyes widen in terror, mine in delight.

"You've hit your head, haven't you?" he asks, barely masking his nervous demeanor with rage, his hand wrapping around my throat. "Maybe you need to go down for a nap?" His eyes are wild and dull, nothing compared to the ocean blue of Alexander's.

One solid, strong hand comes down like a hammer against Mason's shoulder. Alexander rips him away from me. "Take your grimy hands off of my fiancé, now!" he growls, his eyes narrowed while he expertly tosses Mason to the ground, as if he weighed nothing at all.

I watch their violent tousle with worry. What if Mason hurts him?

But now that I see the two men side by side it's like night and day. Mason is shorter, his shoulders less broad than his twin's. Alexander's muscles are more defined, and he's taller, much taller.

He's stronger, too.

Douglas steps forward, unsheathing his sword. "The show is over, Mason. You're coming with us."

Alexander pins Mason to the ground, his eyes wild with rage. Then, his fist collides with Mason's face. "How dare you put your hands on Arianna!" He yells, jaw taunt and veiny, as if only a sliver of sanity kept him from going over the edge and ending it all right now. "I'm going to fucking kill you!"

I walk closer to them, knowing this isn't the way to save anyone. Alexander continues bashing his knuckles into his brother's jaw, and I hear bones cracking with every slam.

"Stop! Alexander, your father." I plead. He looks to me, darkness swirling in his irises, flakes of gold and deep black bursting like fireworks. I take a step back, frightened.

As he studies me, the storm calms inside of his eyes.

"Douglas, take him to the cellar. What guards did he have with him during my absence?" Alexander asks, his knuckles bloody and bruised. Every so often, he looks to me, and part of his anger seems to slip away.

"There were three in total." I look to Douglas, shooting him a grin. "Douglas and Cedric for sure, but I don't know the other one. He was smaller, that's all I know." I tell him.

"Baxter?" Alexander repeats to himself, unsure.

Douglas shakes his head. "I'm not sure. The other never spoke nor lifted their shield."

I nod. "I will say, I don't think Cedric meant me any harm, he was just following what he thought was your orders." I peel my eyes from Alexander to send Douglas a look of appreciation. "But Douglas was the one who defied him."

Alexander nods, gesturing to Mason. Douglas grips his shirt tail and drags him upward. Mason is slumped forward but still breathing.

I follow closely behind Alexander as we trail down into the darkest parts of the castle, our footsteps echoing against the empty walls. We wind down uneven stone steps until we reach a cellar of sorts. A heavy, musty odor encircles us. It's almost unbearably cold down here, and we soon reach a room with a singular pendulum light that barely illuminates the area.

"Sit." Alexander orders, but Mason is unable to do much except breathe and try not to fall over at this point. Douglas shoves him down onto the chair and ties his hands with thick twine.

Mason looks up, his face swollen from the beating he received. "Hello, brother." He spits on the ground. His teeth are coated in red and blood dribbles down his cheek.

Alexander lets loose a grim laugh. "Don't call me that. You're cut from the family. Fucking nothing to me."

Mason's demonic laughter sweeps through the frigid, dark space. "What are you going to do Alex? Kill me?" He scoffs.

A deep growl emanates low in Alexander's chest. He doesn't let himself lose his cool here like he did outside, however. Instead, he's swift and steady while he continues his interrogation. "How are you alive?"

Mason shakes his head with a cruel smile. "That's my secret."

Douglas steps forward, towering over Mason. "Do you want me to get it out of him, sir?" His eyes flash with anger and something much more wicked. It seems like he's been wanting this for quite some time.

"No need." Alexander shakes his head. "I'll come back later when Arianna won't be able to witness the terror I'll put him through to get answers to spill from his deceiving tongue." He looks back to me, pleading with his eyes. "Maybe you should go now, love. I don't want you to see this."

I don't know what's more frightening, a snarling, desperate man, or one who seethes quietly, calculated in his actions. Alexander is the quiet one, like a viper waiting to strike.

I shake my head, trying to hold back the chattering of my teeth from the cold. "I'm never leaving your side." I declare, not letting the matter be discussed further.

Mason coos, mocking us. "How sweet, you and your whore."

With a swift movement, Alexander's knuckles collide with Mason's cheekbone. The crunch of bone echoes from the stone walls. "Don't ever speak of her that way." he snarls, shaking out his hand.

Getting back to the matter at hand, Alexander bends down, making eye contact with his brother. "Where is my father?"

"Don't you mean our father?" Mason's maniacal laugh frightens me. Chloe grips my hand, making me jump.

"Where were you?" I whisper to her.

She leans in, her voice barely audible. "I can help."

"How?" Alexander asks, and I'm not sure how he heard her. His attention seems sharp and aware down in this cellar.

"Let me read his mind... the pull of his memories

might kill him though." Chloe says.

Alexander doesn't hesitate, stepping out of the way he gestures to his twin. "Proceed."

She walks close to Mason, who from his expression looks pissed. With her eyes closed, Chloe touches Mason's hair. His face pales as he stares sharply at Alexander, a seething glare of hatred floating between them as Chloe pulls the memories from Mason's mind.

When his eyes roll into the back of his head, I fear he will die and we will never know the location of the King, but she releases her hand and his lungs fill with damp air as he coughs, catching his stolen breath. After a beat of silence, she speaks. "He's at the cabin."

"What cabin?" I ask, imaging there must be hundreds in the forest.

Alexander looks to me and shakes his head, advancing on Mason before I can stop him. "Who told you about the cabin?" he demands.

A sinister grin creeps onto Mason's face. "Does it matter?"

Alexander's wild eyes dart around the room. "Your thoughts are not safe, and neither is your truth. We hold power over both, Mason. You've lost, so quit biting your fucking lip and own up to your failure." He spits, grabbing my hand in his and leading us swiftly away. For a moment, he looks back to his brother one last time. "Useless,"

As we exit the cellar, Alexander is quiet, hell-bent

on going to whatever cabin they were speaking of. My thoughts, however, shift to my little sister and her safety.

With Chloe trailing close behind I turn my head, trying to read the faces of those around me. "How's Mia?"

"She's okay! They're having a great day." She grins, her positive demeanor helping to dismantle the heavy, grim fog that seems to grip us all.

Alexander's large hand covers his face, and he pulls it down to look at me. "I can't wait to meet her. I'm so sorry about all of this. Your welcoming to Haven was supposed to be the exact opposite."

Gripping his hand, I flash a reassuring smile.

Chloe places her hand on top of ours. "Do you want me to take us there now? The cabin, I mean."

Alexander nods, his expression haunted when he looks to me. "This isn't how I wanted you to see it." he says.

"See what?" I ask, confused.

"The cabin." He glances up at the pink sky. "I built it for you years ago because I wanted us to have somewhere to go ... just the two of us."

I touch his face, trying to melt away his stress. "This will all be over soon, okay? We can spend as much time there as you'd like. Let's go get your dad, for now."

When he agrees, Chloe's grip strengthens on our hands. I close my eyes tight until she speaks again. "This is as far as I can take us." she announces.

The sunset gleams upon the waves splashing at the sand beneath my feet, water playfully dancing near, but never quite reaching us. I've never been to this side of the castle, nor have I ever seen Haven's ocean up close.

When I turn my head, I see a forest sprawling with life. Birds chirp above our heads, and small creatures scamper within the brush, piquing my curiosity. Light peers in through the trees, inviting us inside.

There aren't any words spoken when Alexander covers my hands in his before leading me to a small trail up ahead. With that, we descend deep into the quiet woods. Chloe and I both have trouble keeping up with his long, swift strides, even as I hold his hand in mine.

"You're probably wondering why she didn't take us directly there, aren't you?" he finally asks.

I nod. "A little, yeah."

"The cabin and surrounding woods have been enchanted." Alexander smirks. "I wanted this to be the one place that felt like home to you, somewhere we could go to escape. No magic allowed."

He's good. So, so good.

"I don't deserve any of this." I say softly, wondering what I ever did to make him love me so much.

"You do, and we're almost there. Keep holding my hand and come with me to meet the King, your future father-in-law."

We continue our journey. Fluffy moss lays beneath

my feet as I allow the ugly dress to flow and get covered in dirt and leaves while I walk. "I've got to change soon." I sigh.

"But that dress is so pretty." I can sense the sarcasm in his voice.

I laugh. "Only the best for your brother," I joke, but Alexander squeezes my hand, holding a protective glint in his eyes.

Chloe chimes in after I almost forgot she was behind us. "If Alex didn't enchant this place, I could change you whenever." She sticks her tongue out at him.

"How much farther?" I question, getting more nervous about the state of his father's health the farther we descend into this desolate wooded area.

Alexander grits his teeth. "Only a few more minutes. Chloe, did he look harmed in the vision?"

She shakes her head. "I didn't see him, I only saw Mason locking the cabin door. But I could hear the King yelling."

Her words linger in the air as we walk in silence until we approach the clearing where the cabin sits. A rush of calm washes over me when I realize that we're one step closer to this nightmare being over.

Alexander's body stiffens as we stand in front of the quiet cabin. "I'll check it out. Stay here." he announces, but it's more of an order. He's understandably on edge.

"I'm coming." I say and Chloe agrees. We creep

towards the cabin with slow, nearly silent steps, aside from the occasional crunch of a leaf or twig, of course. Despite nerves messing with my stomach, I can't help but admire how beautiful the scenery is.

Before us stands a deceptively serene cabin, one made of light wood and brick. Moss and ivy climb up its sides, and rose bushes entice us closer. Nearby, a deer munches on some grass at the edge of the forest surrounding the cabin, unaware that we're even here. I'd imagine that inside is something just as homey as the outside, with leather furniture and plaid blankets.

If circumstances were different, I'd be ecstatic to find something like this in the woods. I might even want to live here, too. The only strange thing I can see is the smoke puffing from the chimney, despite the warm weather that holds Haven in its grasp today.

"I see him!" Chloe yells excitedly, peeking through the front window.

Alexander looks in, his hands cupping the glass. "That bastard," He curses his brother. When I look, I can't help the gasp that escapes my lips. The king is tied to a chair near the door, something covering his mouth.

His eyes widen when he sees us peeking in. "Dad, are you okay?" Alexander asks his father.

His father violently shakes his head, but we can only hear muffled sounds coming from him.

Alexander looks around the area frantically, but

once I grab the door handle and see that it's unlocked, I calm. "Look! We can go in." I squeal.

I turn the knob and step inside before Alexander screams at me to stop. But it's too late, as I've already made the mistake of thinking this would be a simple rescue mission.

My dress is instantly covered with splatters and drops of thick red blood. "Oh my God!" I cry out. Alexander rushes in beside me and checks my shaking body. "I'm so sorry," is all I can say as I take in the violent scene around me.

"Dad!" Alexander bellows, the desperation in his cries breaking my heart. My knees collapse next to Alexander's father as realization hits me of what happened.

When I opened the door, a mechanism was turned on, resulting in a pointed, sharp piece of glass impaling the king's ribcage. Alexander's strong resolve breaks, and tears stream down his face when he takes in the horrific sight.

"Alexander ..." I cry out as he fumbles with the heavy chains, trying with every bulging muscle to rip them apart.

I apologize again, nearly frozen where I stand.

"It wasn't your fault; it was a trap, and we have to get him out of here, now!" he yells, breaking me out of my trance.

I find the king's wound and carefully place my hand firmly over the areas without glass, knowing that if I pull out the massive shard, he will bleed out even faster than he is now. "His pulse is weak." I croak, my brain going into overdrive. How could I be so stupid?

Chloe's frantic voice pulls me from my self-loathing. "Umm, guys. We have another problem." Her finger points to the fireplace where a cauldron above the fire is spitting out molten flames onto the rug.

"Ari, go!" Alexander pleads. His bloodied hands grip my face while he orders me to leave him in the swirling orange and red that is quickly engulfing the wooden cabin. "I said go!" he roars.

The ferocious, crackling sound of burning wood ignites around us. "I'm not leaving." I let my words be known with an unusual deafening order in my tone. This is what I do: help people. The next logical step is to pick the chair up, but its large wooden feet are bolted to the ground.

"Chloe, take him ..." Before Alexander can finish, realization dawns on his perfect face. There's no way for Chloe to help.

No magic here.

Not in our enchanted cottage that's tucked away in the forest. Our safe haven has become a bloodied death trap.

And it's all my fault.

THIRTEEN

The fire continues to crackle and engulf everything in its path. Flames have completely taken over the back side of the cabin.

Alexander rushes to the front porch. He brings his fingers to his mouth and a loud whistle escapes his lips, one echoing through the forest around us.

"Chloe, go find help." I cough through the thick, black haze that has begun to suffocate everything inside.

Alexander rushes back in, smoke fuming around him. "If you're not going to leave, I'm forcing you out." With strong but gentle arms, he throws me over his broad shoulder against my tears and protesting.

I try to reason with him, my voice cracking. "I have to manage the bleeding, and you have to put me down!" I fall into a fit of violent coughs. Black smoke puffs from the front door and into the fresh air when he sets me outside.

"Your horse will be here in a moment, and I need you two out of this fucking cabin, now!" His raised voice alarms me; I'm already frantic from this dire situation.

"You can't do this alone." I plead, trying to come up with a solution but all my mind can think of is red. Blood is mixed with black soot everywhere.

Gallops take over and I look forward, smiling when I see Cloud heading steadfast towards us. "I'm not doing it alone." Alexander gestures to the magical 'horse,' as he calls him.

Once Cloud is in front of me, seeing him makes me calm. For a moment, Alexander is confused by my familiarity with the unicorn until he realizes his wedding gift was already given to me.

Alexander disappears from sight, returning a moment later with an axe. I watch on helplessly from the front yard as he grips the handle and brings it down with power, smashing the wooden legs of the chair. I cheer when they split in half.

"Hurry!" I shout.

They both move quickly as Alexander breaks the rest of the wood that's in his way and he pulls the chains through, removing the barrier that his father desperately needs to escape from. He hoists the king over his shoulder.

Violent coughs erupt from Alexander's lungs when he exits the cabin.

"Lay him on his back." I instruct. He lays the king down gently against Cloud's soft fur and wraps rope around him. He turns and picks me up, setting me behind his father.

"Go!" Alexander shouts, and Cloud starts to move.

I begin to question my strength, so I call back, "What if he falls?"

"I tied him. Just hold the wounds and go to the castle." he instructs, trusting me fully with his father's life as he steps back.

"Go, Cloud!" I take one last look while we take off through the forest. Alexander is broken, his glistening eyes gazing at me as we rush off.

Behind him, the cabin he built for us crumbles at his feet, the flames reaching the tips of the massive trees. I look down, holding the limp hand of the king, Alexander's father, and my future father-in-law, and mutter the only words I can think of, "I'm going to save you."

I let out a breath when I feel him squeeze back. It's weak, but it's a comforting sign that he can hear me.

"Please move!" I yell to the guards that stand at the edge of the castle. They bow when they see me and just as quickly, they rush to my side when they see their king hanging over and blood dripping from Cloud's white fur. "The king, he's hurt. I need to fix him!"

The heavy metal doors are opened, and more

guards arrive with a stretcher. "Come with me. The infirmary is this way," A knight tells me.

I brush my fingertips against Cloud's soft fur, thanking him for getting us to the castle so quickly. "Oh, honey! You're covered in blood." Pen rushes out, with Ruby not far behind her.

"I'll fetch your clothes. What do you need?" Ruby asks, her eyes carefully wandering over the king's body as he lays on the stretcher.

"The clothes don't matter. What kind of tools do you have in the infirmary?" I ask, my tone clipped. I'm not annoyed with them, I'm simply mad at myself.

"Everything you need, princess." She bows, and I wish she didn't. I don't deserve their kindness; I did this.

The corridor seems to stretch on forever as we make our way to the infirmary.

I ignore the unfamiliar paintings of people I've never met, along with the anxiety I feel about this situation. My sister is off who knows where, and I feel responsible for creating this horrible situation. It is all too much to bear. "I hope I can save him." I gasp.

Penelope lays a gentle hand over mine. "You will, I just know it." she assures me, and I wish I believe her.

"It's my fault." I stutter, and the women give me an odd look. Not understanding my words, but not questioning them either.

We step into the infirmary and I pay close attention

to the tools placed on the counter. The guard from earlier walks over to me. "Anything else you need?" he asks.

"Someone to help. Someone with experience," I tell him.

"I'm here!" I turn to see an unfamiliar woman in mid bow, her hair curly and wild. "Hello, princess." she says.

I shake her hand, covering her in blood without realizing it. I'm still in shock but I need to be completely aware for this. "No need for any formalities. I'm Arianna, and it's nice to meet you."

Despite our cordial conversation, we operate in full swing.

We wash our hands, and the woman begins sterilizing the tools. I place an apron over my bloodied dress, thankful that I have someone to help. I'm not a doctor, but maybe she is. "Are you a doctor? I didn't catch your name."

"It's Willow." She smiles. "I'm a healer."

"Perfect." I grin, thankful for the help and recognizing her name from the wedding gift. "Here, I'm going to remove this glass. I need you to rea—" she stops me with a hand and a gentle expression.

"Princess, I mean no offense, but I understand. I know what you're going to say without having to say it." I touch my pendant; she smiles at the movement. "I can't read your mind, darling. I'm just good at what I do."

I send her a smile, but my nerves don't let it reach my eyes. Pen and Ruby usher everyone out of the room. "I hope this didn't hit an artery; god, I hope it didn't."

The room is so quiet that one could hear a piece of cotton collide with the ground as I pull out the long, thick shard. Willow is on standby with gauze. A breath of relief washes over me when the sharp edge finally exits his body and blood doesn't spurt out.

"Oh, thank Haven!" Willow breathes. "I'll clean. You can get ready to stitch."

I nod, trying to steel my shaking hands. Normally, when someone is injured, they come to me. Normally, I don't witness the terror they go through beforehand.

Normally, I'm not the one responsible.

"Ready for you, princess." Willow says.

I shake my head. "Please, call me Ari." She doesn't miss the tremble in my voice or the shaking in my hands as I bring the needle to his skin.

"Here, Ari." Gently, she lays her hand over mine. "I've got this, why don't you bandage the other wounds?"

I sigh with relief. "Thank you." I tell her. I now have a moment to quiet my mind while I focus on cleaning and bandaging his other cuts. I watch in awe as Willow expertly, and without fear, stitches up her king.

"Do you do this a lot?" I wonder.

"Oh, yes. One particular prince made me very good at stitching. I believe you know him, too." She winks, easing my mind with her calm demeanor. "Alexander likes to get into trouble, and I'm always the one to fix him. It's a good thing his heart belongs to a healer." she chuckles, nudging me with her elbow once she finishes.

"Trouble?" I ask, only imagining what he must get into.

"Oh, definitely. Aside from his battle wounds, he has a tendency to get into tousles." She laughs to herself, reminiscing on a faraway memory. It doesn't come as a surprise; Alexander has a tough exterior.

We step back and Willow admires her work. "You did wonderful, Ari." she tells me.

"Me?" I croak, checking the king's pulse and smiling when I notice how much healthier it sounds. "It was all you. I completely failed him."

Willow harbors the kind of warmth that can melt a frozen tundra. "Darling, look at you. Covered in blood and shaken up by whatever happened. Don't blame yourself; it was never your fault."

The sound of heavy boots stomping down the corridor echoes against the stone walls. "How is he?"

"Oh, Alexander." I collapse into his arms, feeling like the weight of the world has left my shoulders the moment his arms wrap around me. "He's stable. Willow said—"

Willow walks over to him, and I can't help but find her tiny compared to his tall frame. "He'll be just fine, Alex.

Arianna here saved him. Without her, I'm not sure what would have happened."

I want to correct her, but the way Alexander's eyes lovingly roam my face makes me go quiet.

"Thank you." he says softly, but his body doesn't calm. "Both of you."

Willow gestures to the door. "Now head along. I'll stay with him."

I shake my head, not wanting to go. "It's okay. Really,"

Alexander walks to his father's bedside and gently places a hand on his shoulder. "She's right. We need to wash the blood from our bodies." His voice travels through the room, although it's barely above a whisper. The room goes still while he prays over his father's unconscious body.

Leaving the infirmary, Alexander places his arm around my back as we walk to the mob of people impatiently waiting to hear about Haven's leader.

Everyone crowds around, and it almost seems that no one is willing to take a breath until Alexander speaks. "He'll be fine." He breathes. I can feel the tension of the people immediately melt away over the good news. What's incredible is that there's no questions; they'll never know of the horror we witnessed, and Alexander will always put on a brave face. It's admirable.

"We're going to our room, no disturbances." he

announces, making sure to send a warming smile, although I know inside, he's crumbling.

As the crowd dissipates, my eyes wash over the leaving visitors looking for pink hair, not wanting to go without making sure Mia's okay. "Chloe?" I call out.

I catch a pop of her bright ponytail. "Yes?" She glides forward, a radiant aura around her as always. I wish I was okay, but right now I'm just not, and I don't need Mia to see me like this.

"I need to rest." I tell her. "Could you check on Mia? Maybe hang out with her for a while?"

"On it!" she sings, dancing out of the room.

Finally, we make our exit down a dark and quiet hallway. The castle is surprisingly still—minus the guards, of course. They don't speak, but they shuffle around the halls. Alexander guides me up a long staircase, and I grip the aching tension in my arms, the anxiety of the past two days' hectic events starting to get to me.

I take a calming breath to steady myself, not wanting to bring it up, but also needing to know, "What about Mason?" I ask him as we round another hall.

His thumb gently rubs circles on my skin, causing chills to shoot through my body. "You're shaking." is all he says.

"I'm just so scared." I mutter, feeling my lips tremble.

He pinches the bridge of his nose in frustration,

eyes shooting daggers at the ground while we walk. "It was never meant to be ... like this."

"Please," I stop him. Nearby, flickering flames encased in a glass fireplace illuminate the halls, creating a golden hue atop his already tan skin. "It's your father on that table, Alexander. Don't worry about me."

Alexander lifts his hand to hold my chin, gaze full of concern. "It's my job to worry about you."

The strong scent of butane from a wall lantern invades my nostrils and instantly, the burning scent of wood dominates my thoughts, reminding me of our cabin that I never got to know.

Alexander senses the change in my mood.

Placing his warm hand on the small of my back, he guides us to a door at the end of a hall. "Let's go relax in the bath, my love. I need you." His tone is sultry and full of want. "I need you to distract me."

FOURTEEN

I step inside and try to appreciate the impossible fact that I'm standing here with the man from my literal dreams.

"Is this your room?" I ask, looking around at the interior. A large, canopy bed colored with crimson blankets and stunning brown furs sits flush against a long wall. From the bed, one could easily view a balcony fit with frosted floor-to-ceiling glass doors.

Polished marble flooring sits below my feet, and atop it stands velvet furniture strewn about with a sincere attempt at organization. Lanterns illuminate the space scarcely, and moonlight dances upon the remaining shadows to an almost romantic song.

"It's ours." He replies, melting my resolve completely.

Alexander leads me into a bathroom and opens French doors to reveal the glorious scenery outside, and I'm surprised by the addition of a second balcony. I imagine how refreshing it would be on a spring morning to open both sets of doors in order to allow a gentle breeze to consume the room.

But the thought doesn't settle me, my mind not allowing me to think too long on something as simple as a relaxing morning.

"How are you so calm?" I ask, my fingertips trailing on the soft, smooth stone of the countertops.

"I'm used to blood and gore; I'm a soldier, after all." he replies, his eyes trailing somewhere far away. "I will admit, only to you, that seeing my father in that state shook me up. But I never doubted for a second that he wouldn't pull through."

I nod in agreement. "He seems like a strong man."

Alexander lets out a low chuckle. "Oh, he is. But you are the reason I wasn't worried, Ari."

"Me?" I ask, eyes widening.

With a piercing gaze, he slices through me. "Of course. I knew you'd fix him. Just like you fixed me,"

I laugh a little. "How could I have fixed you? I'm the broken one, and you're a prince," I tell him. Then my face grows somber and my chest tighter. "I'm the reason he got hurt. I shouldn't have barged into the cabin like that. I should have waited for your orders." I mutter.

He wipes away a fresh tear as it slides down my cheek. "You were just trying to save him. It's okay now," Alexander assures me, wrapping me in his arms and pulling me against his solid chest. "I've got you."

Releasing me, he bends down to turn on the faucet to the tub. It's a large, claw-style bathtub. The stonework is like nothing I've ever seen before. It appears to be carved out of quartz. It's beautiful.

A beat of silence passes through when he dims the lights.

When I meet his eyes, he sends me a smirk. "And I know you're not the type of woman to take orders." He smiles, looking me up and down with a feverish glint. "But maybe in ... *other* instances you will?"

I blush at his remark, and my cheeks redden further when his hands land on the sleeves of my dress. "Let's get you out of that thing." he whispers, eyes alight with a passion I've never experienced before. Not this close, and not like this. It makes me feel alive.

I nod, looking up at him with adoration and lust.

"I'd love that." I say, feeling heat rise to my skin at his touch. The way he's looking at me showcases the need and want inside of him, too.

His hands hover over my skin in anticipation, and gently, he starts to unbutton the back of my dress. The soothing feeling of his fingertips contacting more and more of my body sends shockwaves through me, but it feels so good.

"So soft," His breath hits my neck and I gasp, leaning into his touch.

"Alexander ..." I moan. My breathing is irregular, my heart pounding like crazy.

"I've waited so long for this." Alexander says gruffly, his fingers pressing firmly against me. The deep baritone in his voice makes me crave to hear him speak more. Heavy, warm steam fills the bathroom as my disastrous dress hits the floor. "Perfection." he adds, eyes roaming over my body when I turn to face him.

A flit of nerves rises in my stomach and I blush, covering myself with my hands. "Now you." I grin sheepishly.

"As you wish." Alexander smirks.

He slips off his clothes, piece by piece, as we gaze at each other, ignoring what the blood on everything means and simply getting lost in the moment.

Tan, muscular arms pull me close.

The room is entranced in a dim, golden hue as I take in the black ink of his tattoo, unable to distinguish any fine lines. He grips me harder, abs like marble against my cool skin.

"Shall we?" he asks, and I nod.

I expect us to get in the bath, but it's not yet filled. Instead, we step into a walk-in shower that sits to our right. He flips the handle, and we step under the showerhead when it releases water like summer rain.

"I figured this would be better." he breathes. I take in a sense of relief as the water washes away the red blood from my body, allowing myself the comfort of getting lost in Alexander's blue eyes.

He takes his strong hands and splashes the hot water onto my neck, making sure I don't have a speck on me with a firm yet gentle scrub from a loofah. I do the same for him. Once our skin is free of the violent events of the day, we step onto the cool tile floor, forgoing towels.

His lips gently pepper my neckline as we walk, dripping water, towards the tub.

A wooden line filled with glass vials of all different colors sits in a case on a marble-slabbed table beside the tub. Alexander grips a light purple one and drips the contents into the crystal water. A fragrant scent of calming lavender fills the bathroom.

Looking at the cool stone of the tub, I fear the water will be freezing, since it's made entirely of clear quartz, thus making the tub resemble a giant bowl of crystal ice. But it's the opposite as I sink my feet inside.

I'm breathless from the heat of the moment, sinking into the warm water and letting it cascade over my body as Alexander climbs in behind me. I'm facing away from him, with only my back exposed to his gaze. Warm water drapes my chest and I open my relaxed eyes to see him cupping the warm water in his hands and pouring it over my exposed breasts.

"I want to ravish you, Arianna." His lips trail across the nape of my neck. The oils are soft, making our bodies rub against each other smoothly.

"I want you, too." I tell him. Firmly, his hands grip my chin, turning my face to meet his, darkness swirling in his eyes.

He looks feverish, focused. "Don't tempt me, Arianna Castelle. I have to keep control of the situation."

"Why?" I raise my brow, but he doesn't answer. Instead, his full lips crash into mine. Years of longing collide, and sparks shoot through my core.

"Don't control yourself." I beg him through our passionate embrace, and I can feel his hardened length against my back.

His large hands grip the side of the tub for a few seconds, and in what looks like a 'screw it' moment, his hand begins to glide from the nape of my neck to one of my breasts. His thumb glides over my nipples, and he teases them until they harden under his fingertips.

All the while, his lips move between mine and my neck. I moan as his hand easily glides down my skin, smooth from the lavender oil, and a gasp escapes me when his fingers sensually dive into me. Slowly, he works them in and out as he whispers into my ear. "There's things you don't know, things you don't understand about me."

"Alexander," I breathe his name, not

understanding.

The heat rises in my core as his thumb gently strokes my clit, igniting a fire between us. His other hand greedily cups my breast, and every so often he gingerly pinches my nipples.

I feel his breath against my neck. "Let go, Arianna." he demands softly.

I'm writhing beneath him as his fingers work magic inside of me ... but I'd prefer something else. "I need you, Alexander."

He squeezes my clit gently between his forefinger and thumb, not responding to my pleading words. I repeat myself and his fingers slide in and out, causing a passionate moan to escape from my lips. "I could do this all day." Alexander teases, enjoying my undoing.

The pure adoration in his tone makes me squirm. "Please. Take me," I beg, loving this playful, erotic moment we're sharing.

"Let go, I said." His tone is light, playful. He smiles against my neck, and I moan when his finger trails my flower while his free hand travels through my hair.

I nod, leaning my body against him.

I'm not sure why he doesn't want to have sex yet, but what he's doing to me in this moment feels so extravagant that I can't imagine anything would be better than this. My body begins to shake as his fingers sink deeper inside of me.

Alexander's tongue glides softly along my neck until he peppers kisses on my earlobe. "Do you like this, Arianna?" he asks, his voice deep.

"Y—yes," I stutter, melting when a low growl escapes him.

His hard length presses into my back and I can't contain the sounds that escape me when I collapse into him. A wave of pleasure cascades over my body, the most intense experience I've ever had, and at the hands of the man I love.

As I turn my body towards him, water escapes the sides of the tub and splashes onto the tile floor. "Can we go to the bed?" I suggest, my eyes roaming over his face. I tangle myself into him further, wrapping my legs around his body.

Alexander's hands rise out of the water to move the hair from his face. "I ... I can't." he says. I can see behind his ocean blue eyes that he's fighting within himself, but I don't know why.

"Why?" I frown slightly, trying to understand his rejection. "Do you not want me?"

He cups his hands in the warm water and brings it to my shoulders, the water flowing down my flushed skin. "There's things you don't know about me." Alexander's tone is serious, and he buries his face in my chest. "I could hurt you."

I tilt his chin up and take his throbbing length in

my hand.

"I'm okay, I'm ready for you." I promise, blushing.

I'm surprised by my own words, having never been with a man in that way but knowing this is what I want, all the same. I've gone through every base, except the final one. But I've imagined for almost a decade how it would be with him.

Alexander shakes his head, his black hair falling into his face. "It's not about that." he replies, groaning when I stroke him. I can see his resolve faltering, and my lips hover over his before his hand wraps around the nape of my neck. Before our lips touch, he whispers, "You're really testing a man who has no patience, Ms. Castelle."

Delicious chills trickle down my spine at his words.

"I'd love to learn what happens before, during, and after this test." My voice is different, tempting.

With a smirk, he stands up in the tub with my legs still tangled around him. Water overlaps the sides of the tub and spills onto the tile floor when he steps out, carrying me to the bedroom. We're soaking wet and locked into a passionate kiss.

"You belong here," he growls, tossing me gently onto the plush comforter. "And these belong open."

My heart thunders in anticipation as he slides in between my legs. Meanwhile, my fingers dive into his wet, tousled hair as his warm lips glide over my stomach, my arms, my legs.

"I'm going to try ..." Alexander mutters to himself, shaking his head. I don't understand what's going on, but I don't question it. "Stay still." He orders softly.

His lean frame hovers over me, muscles constricting. I place my hand against his marble abs and watch in awe as he takes his large, thick length into his palm and begins stroking it.

His eyes boring into mine and he nods once, biting his lip as if to steady himself and focus.

"I'm ready." I tell him.

He brings the tip to my opening. One hand on himself, the other on the mahogany wood headboard.

"You look so perfect." His velvet voice sings. I feel the slightest buildup of pressure, and then the sound of wood cracking above me. I look to the noise, surprised to see Alexander's fist clutching a missing chunk of wood from the headboard. The remnants of thick wood fall to the bed from his hands. "I fucking knew it." he scolds himself, jumping off of me in seconds, refusing to touch me when he grabs a towel.

"What happened?" I sit up, wrapping the comforter around my body and looking over his face. "What was that? Alexander, you knew what?" I ask.

He paces the room, his body glistening with water. "Get dressed. I'll show you why you're too fragile for me."

Fifteen

I lay against Alexander's bare chest, still reeling that I calmed him down enough to lay with me. "Just tell me what's going on." I plead.

He shakes his head; his fingers twirling my damp hair. "I need to show you, love."

"Show me, then. Just don't get upset with yourself." I tell him, worried. He cracked that headboard in one quick movement, and the wood was at least four inches thick.

"Not here." he replies, sitting up. "We'll go to our clearing."

I stand, not wanting to wait any longer. I place my hand over my necklace, trying hard to understand that this is reality now and no longer my dreams. I have to be more responsible. "We need to see Mia and check on your dad first."

He nods. "I know, and I still have to deal with Mason." Alexander spits his brother's name. "Tomorrow morning, then?" I look to the window to find the twinkling sky swirling with stars.

Silence passes over the room for a brief moment, and I decide that whatever it is, I'll know in time. "What first?" I ask.

"I need to meet Mia." he decides, eliciting a smile from me.

I get dressed, noticing with surprise my unblemished skin.

Earlier, cuts and scrapes adorned my legs and ankles, but now, there's nothing. I continue to rub in confusion until Alexander finally speaks. "You know so much about stones. Didn't you realize what we were bathing in?" he asks, a hint of a grin on his face.

"It's clear quartz." I reply and smile when he grins in approval. I'm intrigued by the look on his face. "So, is it more magical here? Will it fix wounds?" I ask, still rubbing my unscathed legs.

"No, just minor cuts and scrapes. My mom used to tell me it could fix a broken heart." Alexander smiles fondly.

I marvel at the new information.

Natural healing that is amplified by the power that Haven holds. The things this could have done in my world to help. I can't wait to learn more about everything this world has to offer. "Is that true?" I ask, wondering if it will indeed heal a broken heart or if that's one of Haven's quirky myths.

"No. It never worked for me." He frowns, looking out the open balcony doors.

I hate to be jealous, but the thought of him being with someone else and loving them upsets me. "Did you ever get over her?" I wonder, bashfully.

"No fucking way," he responds, and a smirk brightens his features. "It's you."

"I broke your heart?" I gasp slightly.

When he shakes his head, his sharp jawline is illuminated by the candlelight. "No, but the distance did. The constant wonder if I'd ever have you, touch you, take you." he says, dipping his head down. "I remembered words she wrote in her diary, and I tried."

"Well, I'm here now. You never have to worry about that." I assure him with a comforting smile.

We step out into the quiet castle. I was so lost in our own world that I had forgotten just how big this place is and how many live here. Hallways lit with gas lanterns show the way, ones full of elegant paintings, wood-trimmed walls, and plush carpet. Every so often, a guard patrols nearby, never interrupting our stroll.

"Can we trust everyone here?" I ask, nervous there might be others like Mason lurking in the royal shadows.

"Yes, Mason was only here for a few days. All of the guards that were with him during his time here have been apprehended and until I give Mason the serum, I won't be setting them free."

I don't care to ask what 'serum' he's talking about. Instead, I focus on seeing Mia. A guard stands ready at the edge of the stairs, bowing when we approach. "Prince Alexander." He turns to me. "Our future princess, Arianna."

I bow back, not knowing what else to do. Alexander chuckles under his breath, and I have to hold back the playful slap that my hand wants to give him.

"Do you know where Chloe is?" he asks.

The guard's metal arm points down. "Her and a little one arrived here a few moments ago. They're in the dining hall."

We thank the guard and move on, hurrying down the stairs.

"I'm so excited for her to meet you!" I sing, dancing into the dining area. A massive table that could seat around forty people houses Mia and Chloe. She's happily devouring a roast while Chloe sips on a glass of deep purple wine.

"Oh Mia!" I chime, watching as she smiles with delight at the sound of my voice. "I have someone here who wants to meet you."

She rushes over to me, intrigued but a little

frightened. Her green eyes examine as she cranes her neck up to see him. "Al ... Alexander?" She stutters, her hand gripping my jeans nervously.

I bend down to meet her eyes while Alexander steps away, his face looking torn. "It wasn't him, Mia. It was his twin." I remind her.

"They look so much alike." she whispers back.

Chloe walks over, handing me a fresh glass of wine. "Can I talk to you for a minute?"

We walk away to get some privacy. "I can sense how worried you are. She'll be okay." Chloe tells me.

"She was so excited to meet him, and Mason ruined it." I frown.

Chloe brings up her hand, her pink manicured finger gesturing behind me. "I wouldn't say he ruined it."

I look back, and my heart melts.

Alexander's sitting in front of Mia in a chair, talking to her. "And Chloe will make you the biggest princess dress imaginable." He's animated as he talks to her, his hands flying everywhere.

"Really?" she asks, a little skeptical but she can't hide her grin, and Alexander can tell.

"Yes." He nods, fully entrenched in a conversation with Mia discussing all things princess.

Mia grabs a bite from her plate, seemingly comfortable. "Can I have a prince too?" she asks, and me and Chloe chuckle.

Alexander's eyes meet mine, his crooked grin melting my heart. "One day, many, many years from now."

With Mia happily tucked away in bed, I follow Alexander to the chamber that Mason is confined in. Douglas is standing guard, ready for us to arrive.

"I've got the Candor." He tells Alexander, placing a vial full of bright blue liquid into my prince's palm.

"What is it?" I ask, trying to examine the liquid and coming up empty.

He holds it up, tilting the glass to its side. Bubbles pop and move inside the vial. "A truth serum. It will make him tell all." Alexander replies.

Mason laughs, spitting on the ground and casting us all a deep, menacing glare. "Go ahead. Nothing can stop me."

Alexander doesn't bother with small talk. Instead, he shoves the bottle right into Mason's mouth and waits until the last drop is down his throat before stepping back.

The room is lit by golden candles, and a warm ambience casts a shadow against Alexander's hard edges. He looks refined, muscular, and unstoppable. I look to his twin, who is staring back at me with a sinister smile. For a moment, I'm afraid, but then I remember Alexander is by my side, forever ready to protect me.

Alexander crosses his arms, planting his feet into the ground. "Why are you here?" he asks.

"To marry her." Mason responds, nodding his head in my direction.

Alexander's fists clench at his sides, but he continues. "For power?"

Mason laughs, the sound making me cringe. "Of course, brother. Why else? I was going to marry her, and then kill father so I would become king." His eyes pan to me and he frowns. "Tragically, she would die the night of our wedding. It's a shame I didn't get to—"

"Don't finish that fucking sentence." Alexander barks, jaw rigid with rage.

Mason rolls his eyes. "Anyways, do what you will. I'm getting bored." He yawns, infuriating me.

"How could you hurt your own father?" I demand, hands trembling at my sides as anger catches hold of me. I step forward but Alexander stops me, Mason's maniacal laughter echoing off the walls.

"Hurt? He's alive?" Mason frowns, his disgusting plan having not been executed upsetting him.

Alexander smiles. "Arianna saved him."

"How... sweet." Mason draws the words out after some effort, face showing he thought it was anything but. If he wasn't chained down, I could imagine him flicking dirt out from underneath his fingernails.

Alexander pulls his hands behind his back, stiffening and demonstrating a military stride as he continues his interrogation. "How are you alive?"

Mason bites his lip, but the serum is too powerful. "You never killed me. You just thought you did."

Alexander nods, taking in the new information with a stoic expression. "Who helped you?"

Mason again clenches his teeth, but it doesn't hold. "Bestan and Laurent." The words fly from his mouth and the guards in their cells nearby groan from being called out.

Alexander nods. If the information fazes him, I wouldn't have been able to tell by his cool demeanor. "No one else? Cedric?"

Mason shakes his head. "No one else."

I chime in, curious. "Can we trust him?" I ask.

"The serum is absolute." Alexander replies, then he turns to Douglas. "Kill him and his accomplices."

"Yes, sir." Douglas nods.

Alexander gently grabs my arm, leading us away. Just once, he turns his head back to look at his brother one final time. "Goodbye, Mason."

I can see his brother look up through narrowed eyes. "See you in hell, Alex."

SIXTEEN

Morning light filters in through the bedroom windows, a warm breeze hugging our bare bodies while we lay in the canopy bed. Fresh air can do wonders for your soul, so we slept with them open last night.

Alexander turns to me, his blue eyes drinking me in. "You look gorgeous in the morning," he says. I turn from him to blush in peace, but his fingers grip my chin.

We're tangled in the sheets, having spent our first night together. But no matter how hard I tried; Alexander wouldn't make love to me. It's not something I've done before, but with him ... I so badly crave to feel his touch in that way.

"Can we go to the clearing now?" I impatiently ask, my fingers trailing on his chest around a particular tattoo that I wasn't able to fully make out in our heated moments yesterday.

He looks to the ceiling, unsure. "I don't want you to hate me."

"I could never hate you." I assure him, but he shakes his head.

"I'm scared that when you find out, you'll run." He kisses my forehead. Taking a moment to brush the hair from my face. "Your scarlet hair is like fire."

I smirk. "Don't try to change the subject." I giggle when he tickles me.

He shrugs. "Doesn't matter what I want. We have more important matters to attend to right now."

We had checked on his father last night to find that he was asleep and healing well, so that couldn't be it. "Like what?" I ask.

His smile lights up the already bright room. "Your formal entrance to the castle. You need to meet our people."

"Like ... today?" I stammer with wide eyes, my breath already quickening. Sheepishly, I tug one of the soft furs accompanying us on the bed to hide my nervous frown.

"Yes. Chloe's already prepared dresses for you and Mia,"

I groan, sinking into the silk sheets. The smell of lilacs wafting in through the windows does little to comfort the uneasy feeling now brewing in my stomach. "What if they don't like me?"

"They've known about you for years. They'll love you. I promise." Alexander shoots me an adoring grin and I inhale, taking in the crisp morning air and chirping birds outside.

"I don't know how to be regal; I trip on my own two feet. I can't rule anything, I just want you." I admit.

He frowns, touching his fingertips to mine. "The crown is a part of me. I can't escape it, even though sometimes I wish I could."

Alexander wears his emotions on his sleeve, so I can see how much it pains him to say that, but it seems that these feelings are only shared behind closed doors when he's around me. Seeing him around others, he is stoic and serious.

"I'll follow you anywhere, I guess I'm just nervous. I mean, I thought I was coming here to meet some guy from my dreams ... not a prince." I giggle.

He smiles, dimples sitting against tan skin. "You'll do great. I'll be right beside you the whole time."

"What about the wedding? Everyone thinks I flaked." I yank a pillow over my face, trying to hide from the pressure. "They're seriously going to hate me." I croak.

"Okay, first off," He rips the pillow from my face. "I can't hear you with that on your face. Secondly ..." He stands, his lean body distracting me from all other thoughts. "You're the most amazing woman I've ever met. If someone hates you, I'll banish them." Alexander shrugs, but I don't know if he's joking.

"That's not a thing, right? Banishing?" I gulp.

"Sometimes." My prince smirks. "But it will be an immediate punishment if anyone so much as looks at you the wrong way."

"Not funny," When I throw a pillow at him, he leans down to kiss me. "Tell me about the crest." I gesture to the black ink on his chest.

He places his hand over it, avoiding my gaze. "For my family name. Our family name if you would like." His royal uniform is hung up near the dresser, and he begins to put it on.

"Thane." I say his last name, surprised at how easily it rolls off my tongue. How right it feels.

"Alexander Hayes Thane." he proclaims with a proud expression. He then leans down, pointing at various spots on the crest. "This is our land's animal; a beast of Haven named Wolferen." Alexander states. I look to the black silhouette of the clawed animal that sits in the middle surrounded by a shield. Underneath is a sentence in an unfamiliar language.

"What is that?" I ask, raising a brow.

"The definition of Haven written in an ancient language from our land. 'A place of safety or refuge.'" Alexander replies.

"I love that." I sigh to myself, feeling right at home in this bed, this castle. Anywhere that he goes, I'll follow.

Sitting on the edge of the bed, he trails his fingers against the bare skin on the nape of my neck. "And what is your lineage, Arianna Castelle?"

"Itea," I add, and he quirks his brow at me.

"Interesting middle name. Is it passed down?" he inquires.

"No, my mother just liked it." I look out towards the balcony, trying to recall every memory I have of her so that I never forget, so Mia never forgets.

"How did you lose her?" he asks quietly.

I frown, looking back at him. "She was sick." I don't say anything more. I don't want to go into those horrible details. Just the thought makes my chest tight and my palms sweat.

"I'm sorry. My mother got sick too. There was nothing anyone could do; no amount of magic can fix the toxicity of some illnesses."

So many things we know about each other, and so many we don't.

"I'm sorry." I hold his hand. "Did she enjoy being queen?"

"She was born for it." He laughs at a far-off memory. "Not literally. My father was the heir to the throne. He met her in the village when they were just kids." He smiles wistfully for a moment, memories no doubt flooding his mind like mine had only moments before. "He knew when he saw her that he wanted to make her his bride."

"That's so romantic," I swoon, imagining such young love blossoming into a lifelong commitment tied with a kiss and a promise to not only them, but to Haven.

A knock sounds on the door and Gerardo brings in his tray, stacked to the brim with silver platters covered by domed lids. Artie follows closely behind him.

Beneath the lids reveals a stunning display of poached eggs, bacon, sizzling baked ham and roast beef, bread rolls accompanied by an assortment of jams, and lastly, steaming hot black tea.

My mouth waters at the sight of this incredible feast like I've never seen, but I have to hold back.

Artie still has a job to do.

Nothing could ruin such a perfect breakfast quite like being poisoned, not like that is something I'll get used to anytime soon. Artie bows before taking a knife and cutting into the meal, gulping hard with a dreadful expression, but he does his best to remain as calm as ever.

It's in that moment of him swallowing that I imagine how he feels. Knowing that bite of food might be his last. You can see it in the way his eyes close as the bacon slides down his throat, and the spring of life when a few seconds in, he opens them and a glimmer of hope shines through.

After the tasting, we're left alone to have breakfast on the balcony.

A breathtaking landscape invites gentle conversation, but a nagging feeling looms over me. I can't possibly enjoy this lavish experience while others are suffering. I swallow a piece of the bacon before finding the courage to speak. "I don't like that he has to taste our food." I admit quietly, not wanting to overstep.

Alexander waves it off, continuing to devour his breakfast. "It's precautionary. I promise it's sanitary and necessary."

I shake my head. "No, I mean I don't agree with his punishment."

Alexander raises a brow. "How do you know of his punishments?"

"He told me." I reply cautiously, not wanting to anger him.

His knuckles turn white when he clenches his fist. "If he bothers you, I can find another prisoner."

"No," I break into a smile. "I asked him, Alexander."

"Oh," He nods, taking that in. "What is it about it that you don't like?"

I gulp, not sure how to answer. I decide on the truth. "I just don't see it being fit to his crime. Every single day he wakes up and eats three meals like we all do, the difference for him is every bite is a risk to death."

"He's a criminal." Alexander reminds me.

My hands fidget under the table. "I understand, but do you even know what he did?" Stealing seems hardly a crime for a risk of death.

Alexander scoffs, setting down his glass with a little more flourish than necessary. "Arianna, do you think I would implement a prisoner to a possible death sentence without knowing what he did?"

"Maybe it's not about what he did, but why he did it." I whisper, countering his argument.

Alexander inhales a sharp intake of breath. "I see," A beat of silence passes between us, and I can see the decisions and ideas swirling behind his blue eyes.

I tip my cup of fresh tea and take a swig. "I'm sorry if it's not my business."

His hand covers mine. "No, don't apologize. You're right. It's not fair." He leans back in his chair. "And I want you to tell me things like this. You have every right to make changes as you see fit."

"So, is he going to be freed?" I ask.

Alexander shakes his head, a small chuckle escaping him. "Is there an alternative you can implement immediately?"

I bow my head. "No."

He tilts my chin up. "Then find one, and I will free him."

A grin lights up my features. "Really?" I squeal,

wanting to jump onto his lap.

"Yes." He groans, leaning his head back. "Everyone's going to think I've gone soft."

I shake my head. "No, it's honorable to not rule with an iron fist."

He looks to his own fist. "I don't know how to do that." he admits. I send him a look that tells him he's not alone.

After a break in the heavy conversation, his eyes glance over me. "What was your mom like?" he asks quietly, his tone of innocent questioning so familiar to me from our dreams when we would steal moments to learn things about one another.

I smile while I think of her. "Strong, sweet. She was a nurse, as well. I guess her career choice rubbed off on me."

Alexander nods in agreement. "Willow's going to miss having to fix me up." He grins. The mention of Willow makes me perk up. I already have an idea for how to fix the poison taster situation, and I'll need her expertise for it.

"I really like her! If it wasn't for her, I don't know if I would have been able to save your father." I deflate, starting with a high on my sentence and ending with a devastating blow to my ego.

"That's not true; you're a talented healer. I already heard about your spout with the troll." he chuckles. "And what's your father like? Was it hard to leave him?" Alexander's eyes brush over mine, and a pang of guilt resonates in my chest.

In my dreams, I only brushed the surface of our lives with Frank.

Alexander remembers me living with my mom until she got sick. I didn't want to worry him, and I also thought he was a figment of my imagination. "He's not a good man. It was easy for us to go." My tone is clipped, but I don't mean for it to be.

"I'm sorry to hear that." He sighs, a frown taking over his face. "Do you regret coming here? Do you miss your own world?" Alexander prods, pouring one question after the other.

I sit up from the chair and climb onto his lap. "Not at all, this is where I'm meant to be, with you." I assure him, noting the way his brows are furrowed in worry.

"I just do—"

"Good morning!" Chloe sings. Alexander's unfinished thought is left lingering in the air while she rushes into the room.

"Why didn't you knock?" he groans, running a hand over his face

She appears anxious and in a rush. "Umm, no time! I have to get Ari ready." she squeals.

I giggle as Alexander shakes his head. He turns to me and winks. "I'll meet you downstairs."

Chloe dashes to my side the moment he exits, and her anticipation is palatable. "How was it? Your first night together!" I twirl into the bedroom and plop down on the bed, beaming.

"It was wonderful. He held me all night! I still can't believe this is real. I keep thinking I'll wake up," I admit. A sharp pain makes me wince, and I notice my hair being tugged. I turn to see Chloe holding up a few strands of my hair.

"See! You're not dreaming." she announces.

I grip the sore spot, looking at her with wild eyes. "Where I come from, we pinch." We fall into a fit of giggles.

"Okay, let's do this!" My enthusiastic tone doesn't match the fear I feel inside.

With her pointer finger positioned under her chin, she examines me. "Want me to tell you, or surprise you?" She holds up her manicured finger like a weapon.

"Surprise, definitely." I tell her.

She orders me to close my eyes, and I do as her powers tickle my skin as the silky smoothness of fabric wraps around and hugs my body.

Once my hair moves, I squeal. Chloe laughs, "Almost done! Don't open those eyes!"

"Can we do this like every morning?" I ask, standing on my tip toes.

"Yes!" She beams with pride. The room stills, and

she guides me to the full-length mirror in the bathroom, holding her small hands over my eyes so I won't peek. "Open your eyes, princess."

I gasp when I see my reflection. "Oh, my. I look like Cinderella."

"Cinder who?" She cocks her head, confused.

"A girl from a fairytale. You'll have to read one of them sometime." I smile, knowing we have mine and Mia's storybook fairytales tucked away. I'm so thankful I grabbed them. I touch the soft fabric of the dress, reeling. "Chloe, this is gorgeous!" The blue fabric hugs my body perfectly, and the fluffy skirt creates an ambient drop of silver glitter that cascades into a train behind me. "Mia is going to flip!" I add.

"I already got her ready. She's dying to see you!" Chloe cheers, smoothing out the back of my dress.

I smile. "And my hair," My fingers travel through the loose waves that cascade down my back. Fiery red complements the royal blue of the gown.

Chloe ushers me out of the bathroom. "Are you ready for your entrance?" she asks, pursing her lips as she observes my outfit for any finishing touches.

"No ... yes ... maybe?" I squeak, unsure. She links her arm through mine and we exit the room. "You are so talented, Chloe. I've never seen anyone make such beautiful outfits."

She blushes at the compliment. "Thank you. I'll

meet you down there in a few minutes, okay?"

I fumble for her hands when she retreats. "Wait, no …" I frown, thinking she would have been with me for my entrance.

"It wouldn't be called a grand entrance if you aren't alone." Chloe reminds me.

"But—" I attempt to salvage my nerves.

"No buts," she says sternly with a grin. "It's just Alexander and your sister."

With that, I leave the room and make my way to the staircase where everyone is waiting down below.

I breathe a little easier when my hand brushes the silky wood banister, thankful that it's just those closest to me at the bottom of the stairs. If I fall, it will only be them who see my embarrassment. They wait patiently as I carefully take each step, knowing how clumsy I am.

Alexander's eyes lock on mine, his voice low and rugged as he takes my hand at the bottom step. "Ari," I hear the faintest hint of a growl to his low tone.

"Yes?" I tilt my head, smiling when he opens his mouth to speak but closes it for a moment.

He shakes out of it. "You're so stunningly breathtaking, I can't fucking take it sometimes." he whispers.

"Bad word!" Mia yells.

"Sorry, Mia." Alexander laughs.

I look to my little sister. "Oh, my goodness!" I twirl

her around, getting a good look at her. Her pink dress glistens from the bright lights of the overhead chandelier. "You are gorgeous."

Alexander scoops me into his arms. "Will the prettiest ladies I've ever seen accompany me to meet Haven's people?"

"Yes!" Mia happily claps.

"Yeah," I respond, but the word is filled with worry. I take a moment to straighten the pins on Alexander's uniform.

Alexander leans over, whispering into my ear. "They're going to love you, babe."

My heart pounds when we stand near the open wooden doors that lead out onto a balcony. I can't see below yet, but I can hear the chatter of hundreds. Douglas leans closer to me, "You look beautiful, princess." he says with a reassuring smile.

"Thank you." I tell him while twiddling my thumbs.

"I don't know if I can do this." I admit, hoping Douglas doesn't tell anyone my fears.

"I've got you." he replies in a low voice before coughing. "We're all here for you." he adds.

Mia holds my right hand and Alexander holds my left.

Douglas walks out and stands tall at the edge of the balcony, something resembling a microphone in his hands.

"People of Haven! I would like to present to you," Alexander takes a step forward and I follow.

I gasp when I see everyone looking up to smile and wave at us.

"Our prince, Alexander Thane. Our lovely future princess, Arianna Itea Castelle. Accompanied by Mia Castelle," Douglas announces.

The crowd cheers as Alexander stands stoically tall. With him by my side, looking royal and ready for battle in his uniform, I feel courage.

I wave with a grin as Alexander speaks to his people, suddenly realizing that these are *our* people.

"Hello, Haven." The chattering crowd goes still as they look up to their leader. The way he exudes confidence in not only his stance, but his tone, is striking. "As most of you are aware, our land was under attack." The crowd whispers between themselves. "The king has been injured." Gasps roam below, growing louder. "At the hands of my brother, Mason." The final blow spreads noticeable fear through the crowd.

Alexander sucks in a small intake of breath.

"I will do everything in my power to assure your safety. I know this isn't the news you were looking forward to, but I do have an announcement." Alexander lifts my hand up. "Our wedding is still happening—once my father recovers, of course."

"Are we safe?" someone shouts from below.

Alexander nods. "Mason, and anyone involved in his treason, have been executed. Now we can celebrate my father's health and our future princess coming to Haven."

He turns to me, a proud smile lighting his sharp features.

I lean over the railing, trying to raise my voice loud enough. "Hello," I say. Everyone looks so happy to see me; smiles line the faces between people waving. It takes my breath away and I can't think of anything further to say but luckily, Alexander takes notice.

A few questions sound off, but I can't understand them. My palms are a little sweaty from all the people looking up to me.

With a loving sigh, Alexander snakes his arm around my back. "You'll all have time to meet her soon. For now, we have a wedding to plan." he tells them, and cheers sweep through the crowd. The news of the wedding has boosted moral, for sure.

We retreat inside after waving goodbye to the people, and my hands shake from nerves

"There were like, *so many* people!" At least Mia is calm, as always.

I nod. "Yup, a lot of people."

"You did great babe. Shall we go check on my father?" Alexander suggests, taking my hand in his.

When we make it to the infirmary, I'm surprised to see the king lying awake in his bed. When his eyes catch sight of us, he attempts to lift up. I rush to his side, pleading with him to not reinjure himself. "Please rest, don't sit up."

"Arianna," His voice is hoarse. I reach to the kettle and pour a glass of tea for him.

"It's nice to meet you, sir." I say with a bow.

He chuckles, his laugh warm and inviting. "No need for that, dear. Call me Henry." He looks down to Mia, who is staring back at him with wide eyes. "Who may this be?" Henry cranes his neck to the side and Mia surfaces from behind my legs.

"I'm Mia." she replies shyly.

Henry coughs. "Ah yes, of course. Arianna's sister. Both of you look lovely. How was the meeting?" He turns his attention to Alexander.

"Spirits are high, everyone is comfortable." he tells his father, his hands clamped behind him.

"Good." Henry nods. He opens his mouth to speak but stops himself, looking between me and Mia.

"Come on, Mia, let's let the men talk." I say, readying my sister to leave with me.

Henry reaches his hand out, stopping me. "No, I need you here. I'm just not sure this conversation needs to happen around little ears."

"I see." I look for Chloe, but she's already grabbing Mia's hand.

"Would you like to go to the garden with me and Aurora?" Chloe suggests, a life saver as always.

"Yes, please!" Mia squeals, waving goodbye to us.

Once they exit, Henry sits up, not listening to me when I tell him to stop. Stubborn like his son, I see. So, I help him to sit instead. "Alexander waited so long for you to come here, Arianna, and I'm so sorry Haven wasn't safe for you when you arrived." His voice cracks.

I shake my head, sending a warm smile through the dark atmosphere of the infirmary. I wonder when they'll be able to move him to his room. "Don't apologize. You couldn't have known." I wave off his worries.

"Still, the timing isn't good. My health won't return for a while and I can't lead our people while I'm recovering." He looks away for a moment. Then, his eyes trail to Alexander as I try to understand what he was saying. "The threat?" he asks his son; one can tell the question hurts him. "Has it been eradicated?"

Alexander nods, eyes going glossy with emotion. "Yes, sir."

"Okay." He nods, taking in the information. "Now for the news I'm about to spring on you two."

I fix my posture. "I'm ready to help in whatever way." I promise.

"That's a good thing." Henry replies with a small smile. "Because you and Alexander are now Haven's new leaders, effective immediately."

SEVENTEEN

"How am I going to lead? I can barely take care of Mia, much less an entire country!" I huff, throwing my head back. "Is this even a country? Do you call it a land?" I'm going a hundred miles an hour while Alexander looks calm and collected at my side.

I bury my face in my hands, the overwhelming stress of becoming a queen in a place I'm barely familiar with taking its toll on me. Princess was one thing, as I wouldn't be required to make decisions I have no business making, and still, I was nervous about that.

Alexander places his hands firmly on my shoulders, soothing me as we stand alone in our bedroom. "You're going to do great, Ari."

"What do I do exactly?" I ask, my mind racing.

"I'll handle all military operations, as usual. You, my darling, will handle the duties of the crown. Surveying that our people are happy, perhaps utilizing your skills as a healer to help them." he suggests.

"Okay." I nod, wanting to dive under the covers on our bed and never come out.

We walk to the balcony and he takes a seat on a stone bench, guiding me next to him.

"What is it you fear?" Alexander asks, frowning.

I look out, trying to bask in the sun for a moment while the cool breeze floats through my wavy hair. Briefly, that helps my nerves.

"That I'm not good enough." I admit, trying to not hang my head low. "All my life, I've felt like I was hiding. Just a shell of who I am," I admit, swallowing hard when tears threaten to spill down my cheeks. "Before my mother died, everything was wonderful. But after she passed, everything changed. I always felt a sense of distance in my home and job ...relationships." I hear him sigh at the mention of relationships, but he holds my hand in his silent begging for me to continue. "Nothing I did ever seemed good enough. I felt ..." I try to find the words. "Different than everyone else."

His eyes roam over me. "Do you want to go to the clearing now? I would like to show you why I feel the same way you do."

We walk hand in hand into the clearing from our dreams. Alexander flashes a warm smile as we both comb through our memories of being here together. It's better now, as nothing will rip us apart.

I attempt to let my fears wash away with the wind that sweeps through the tall, blowing grass. I want to learn everything there is to know about this man.

Alexander's haunted expression captures every ounce of my attention. "You really can't leave me, Ari." The desperation in his voice is unusual.

I touch his cheek with my hand, reassuring him. "I won't. Alexander, whatever you're going to show me won't scare me away."

He gingerly removes my hand and walks backward, stepping near the edge of the clearing and standing in front of a familiar, massive, moss-covered rock.

"I don't know why I'm like this." Alexander groans, his fingertips gliding over the moss that's suffocating the stiff rock.

"Like what?" I ask, waiting for him to tell me.

Without warning, his fist collides with the hard stone and the rubble crumbles to his feet. "A monster." he mutters.

I rush to his side, trying to calm his heavy breathing. His blue irises that typically resemble tranquil, clear waters now house a splatter of gold flakes. "Your eyes," I squint to try to see in. His irises appear to go on for miles.

He turns away. "Please, don't come any closer." he begs.

"Look at me!" I demand, unable to let him push me away.

He shakes his head, his jaw clenched. "You don't want to see me like this." he snaps. I grip his face in my hands, angling him in front of me.

"Alexander." I plead.

"Stop." he growls.

I shake my head, hating the way he feels about himself. In a land of magic, he thinks his strength is abnormal? "You're perfect." I tell him, looking into his golden flaked eyes, a pinch of black fog swirling inside of them.

He scoffs, ripping my hands away from him. "I'm perfect? Arianna, I could destroy you with a single touch." he retorts with a sarcastic laugh.

I'm mesmerized by the golden hue in his irises. Wanting to get a better look at his face, I use my finger to tilt him in my direction. He turns to me fully. A haunted twine of black rose like vines sweep underneath his eyes, creating a labyrinth of twisted darkness on his handsome face. "You wouldn't." I say, knowing in my heart that he would never harm me.

Alexander walks away, gripping the trunk of a massive tree and ripping it from the ground. "I'm a monster, Ari." He chucks it across the clearing with ease, never taking his eyes from mine.

"You're the love of my life." I tell him, my tone calm.

He gets down on one knee, diving his hand into the hard dirt. He pulls it back up from the ground, showcasing the mark he left on the solid earth. A full arm's length hole into the soil.

"You're too good for me, too pure." he croaks.

I disagree with a wave of my pointer finger, walking towards him without fear. He takes a step back. "I could hurt you. I can't even touch you properly."

I shake my head. "In the bathtub you didn't."

Although no one is around he steps closer to me and lowers his voice. "Water." he whispers, afraid to let anyone else hear his kryptonite.

"So, you aren't ..." I struggle to find the words. "Powerful in water?"

He nods his head, lingering next to me. "It hinders me." Alexander admits. "Also, the clear quartz."

"So, this is why you haven't ... made love to me?" I breathe, realizing it wasn't about me. He does want me in that way. Of course he does.

"I can't risk it." he says. "I'm broken, Arianna."

I almost laugh at how ridiculous he sounds. "You're far from broken."

With a shake of his head, he grits his teeth. "If I'm

not broken, then why does the bathtub help to hinder me? Water only does so much, but the quartz—" He looks away, breaking off mid-sentence.

An idea pops into my head. "We could in the ocean?" I counter, my mind seemingly in the gutter.

He smirks, his stiff jaw softening for a brief moment. "It's a risk I cannot take, Ari. What if the water isn't enough? I barely trusted myself with the tub surrounding us."

I begin to speak, but he doesn't allow me to.

"Touching you was one thing. Feeling your soft skin against my fingertips was calming. But taking you? Melting our bodies together? It can only be done somewhere without magic."

"Isn't the water magic? It brought me here," I ponder.

"Yes, and I can't explain it, but the magic from the water in Haven is what calms my abilities. It's almost like a medicine."

I nod, realizing the need for our cottage in the woods. "So, the cabin?" A small chuckle escapes my lips when he nods. "You built us an entire cabin, by your hands, for the soul reason of ..." The thought makes me blush.

"I would enchant all of Haven just to have the chance to ravage your body, Arianna." He rolls his bottom lip between his teeth, his mind traveling to the endless possibilities, but he shakes it off. His playful demeanor switches back to despair.

When he doesn't say anything more, I finally ask what's plaguing my mind.

"What are you?"

He paces the clearing, running his hands through his dark, tousled hair. "I don't know. I've been this way since ..." He looks to me, frowning.

"Since when?" I ask.

With a grim look, I see the silhouette of the side of his face. "Since the first night I saw you in my dreams."

Eighteen

"So, it's my fault?" I croak.

He shakes his head, kicking the ground to air his frustrations. "I didn't say that. It's just that when you showed up in my dreams that first time and I tried to come to you, something happened." He looks at me intently, the black vines retreating when I touch his face. "Something changed." He sighs.

"When the darkness came?"

"I think I ..." He looks away, his eyes closing in on the crumbled boulder that he smashed. "It was like it was keeping us apart, you know. And so, every time it pushed, I would pull."

I shake my head. "But it was a dream."

"Can't you see that it was more than that?" He gestures to me standing in front of him in real life. "I brought the darkness back with me. That's how I knew the rose would come back with you."

My eyes gloss over and my voice grows thick with emotion. "Did you ever wonder why the darkness enveloped you?"

A dark expression covers his features. "I allowed it to. I couldn't risk it getting near you. I wanted to protect you." he admits.

I want to stomp my feet, to scream at the endless black pit that made him see himself as a monster.

"At what cost? If you feel this way about yourself now,"

His knuckles brush my cheek. "Ari, I would move oceans for you. I don't care what happened to me now that I've gotten to meet you." He grins. "That's all I ever wanted."

Sadness courses through me at the thought of him being hurt. "If I would have known seeing me harmed you—"

"You're here now." Alexander murmurs into the wind.

I can't help the broken sound that escapes my chest. "But you were in pain all these years, every night."

"I would bottle every ounce of evil in this world and yours, I would endure every tragedy that man has ever faced, just to touch you, to feel you." His fingertips linger along my jawline. His words are poetic and breathtaking and heart wrenching all at once. "There's nothing to fear; the darkness is gone now."

"It's gone because it's inside of you." I sit on the fluffy grass of the clearing, pulling it from the dirt. "What if it hurts you? You know nothing about it."

Alexander kneels beside me, gripping my face in his hands. "Nothing can hurt me, Ari."

"What do you mean?" My brows push together in confusion.

A cocky grin takes over what was once a haunted smile. "Why do you think I lead our military? I can't get hurt now; nothing stops me."

My fingers graze over the crescent shaped scar on the left side of his face. "You've been hurt here." I tell him.

He pauses, quirking his brow. "You didn't see this in your dream?"

I shake my head. "No, I would have known Mason wasn't you. I saw the scar on the painting and thought the canvas must have aged or that the artist didn't paint you correctly."

He nods. "The artist was my mother."

"Oh!" I blush. "I didn't mean that she didn't do a wonderful job." I say quickly, feeling embarrassed.

"I know you didn't." His crooked smile melts me, as usual. He twirls my hair between his fingers. "It makes sense, you not seeing it. Your hair was never this breathtakingly beautiful." He grins. "In real life, it's like an autumn forest when the leaves change into something more."

My skin flushes from the contact of his hands in my hair. I change the subject to calm my heart. "So how can you have that scar and nothing else?"

He shrugs. "That was before I dreamed of you. It was an injury I collected as a child."

I laugh, remembering the healer's words. "Willow did say you were rowdy."

"Exactly. And as much as you are worried about the darkness that lives inside of me, it's made me invincible." I quirk my brow when he says this. "Here." He hands me a blade from his pocket, the silver gleaming against the setting sun.

"What do you want me to do with this?" I ask, trying to return it when he places the blade in my palm.

"Cut me." he says simply, as if that's such an easy thing to do.

I scoff, giving it back to him. "No!"

With a laugh, he grabs the handle of the blade and turns the sharp metal to his wrist. I gasp when he slices into his skin. The blood begins to pour out and along with it, my sanity.

"Alexander!" I grip his wrist, trying desperately to stop the bleeding.

"Ari, look."

I ignore him, my tone frantic. "We have to get you

to the castle; the cut was too deep." I shake my head, realizing we're too far away.

"Arianna!" His stern tone grounds me back to reality. He points down and my eyes travel to where my hands are gripping. Carefully, he peels my fingers away, showcasing his unharmed skin.

"How?" I ask, eyes wide.

He shakes his head, a smirk on his face. "I don't know. No one else does either."

A breath of relief washes over me. "So, you can't die?"

"I heal when I get hurt, but I age, so I'm not immortal. The bigger the injury, the longer I take to heal, but I always come back."

The thought hugs me, knowing I don't have to worry about his safety. "Who knows about this?"

He looks away, as if ashamed. "Douglas and Chloe." he responds.

"Your father?" I press.

Alexander shakes his head, worry plastering his face. "No one else can know. It can put others at risk or worry them. This isn't exactly a normal thing in Haven, to be powered by darkness."

I wonder about me, how I came to be here with him. "Does anyone know how Mia and I were able to come here to Haven?"

"It's hard to explain." my prince appears sheepish.

I remember him saying he was waiting for me at the forest. "How did you know where the portal was? Surely someone knew something,"

His crooked grin melts me. "When an entire town full of magic knows their prince is helplessly in love with a woman from another world, they figure it out. I was eighteen when I started dreaming of you, Arianna. We've had a decade."

I smile, placing my hand in his. "So, it was magic that brought us together?"

"If you can keep the darkness a secret, I think Willow could better explain the passage. Shall we pay her a visit?"

"It's not as simple as magic, it's something more powerful." Willow says, looking between the two of us, her hands tinkering with glass vials set in wooden holders. Alexander and I sit on barstools at the edge of the dark wooden tabletop, listening intently.

I'm waiting on the edge of my seat to hear about mine and Alexander's fairytale story, but my eyes won't stop roaming the endless rows of potions surrounding us. "What is this?" I hold up a green vial in front of me, trying to see the handwritten label.

"That's Porter Potion. It heals a broken heart." She returns it to her pocket, smiling at my curiosity when I pick up another vial to examine its contents.

"I told you she would love it here." Alexander remarks.

Willow smiles. "You're welcome to come by anytime. You could even work with me, if you'd like." The natural healing properties of everything in this shop calls to me.

"I would love that! I could learn all of the potions and ..." Alexander's cough breaks me from my rambling. "Sorry!" I laugh, blanketing my face with my hair. "I got distracted. What were you saying?"

Willow offers us a smile. "What brought you here wasn't magic. It was love; without it, you wouldn't have come here."

Alexander takes my hand. "We're soulmates, Arianna."

Willow nods. "In its purest form."

My fingertips graze the soft wood of the bar top. "So, if that's the case, is there anyone else here from my world?" I ask.

"No, darling. I'm sorry." She pours a purple potion into a glass bottle, and the contents bubble momentarily before dissipating.

A shimmer of glitter catches my eye, and the heavenly-aromatic scent of rose makes me breathe easier. "Is that a love potion?" I ask.

Willow chuckles. "No, this is for you." She hands me the vial.

"What is it?" I raise a brow, taking it in my hands.

"Alexander told me you've had trouble sleeping. This will help."

I look to him, confused. "You've been having nightmares, Ari." he informs me with a concerned frown.

I shake my head; that's impossible. "No, I haven't. The last time I dreamt was when I saw you..." I look away, not wanting to finish the sentence. "When you were hurt."

He touches the vial. "You thrash in your sleep, shouting."

"Oh," I breathe.

Alexander grabs a nearby apple from a fruit basket, sinking his teeth in. "This will help. I used to take it when I had bad dreams as a child."

"So, it will make me have good dreams, or ...?" I wonder.

"It will make you have no dreams, that way your mind can truly rest." Willow chimes.

I put the glass to my lips, the faintest hint of grape lingering on my tongue after I swallow the sweet liquid down.

"I'll have an elixir for you to take each day until your mind calms down." she assures me, but I feel calm. Maybe it's my subconscious that can't rest. I don't feel any different, other than a slight tinge of tiredness, but I suppose that's what a dream potion is supposed to do.

My hand lands on a nearby book. "Should I be

worried that I can't remember my dreams?" I ask, thumbing through the pages while we chat.

"You've gone through so much in a short period of time. It's no wonder your mind is suppressing your memory of your dreams. You'll be fine in no time." Willow promises, her wild hair matching the untamed look of her bookshelf. While the vials are organized, her books are not. They're haphazardly placed on floor to ceiling shelves, and I have a desperate need to organize them alphabetically.

I walk over, letting my fingers graze the bound, aged leather of a few ancient texts.

"Take the blue one home." Willow gestures to the large, tattered royal blue book on the far left. I grab it off the shelf and flip through a few of the pages. Tonics, potions, elixirs.

"I would love to learn some things." I say quietly as I immerse myself in the lettering, trying to find the one thing that's on my mind, my first job as princess of Haven, or now, queen.

"You don't just need to learn it, darling. You need to know every detail from front to back." She grins.

I lift my brow and she walks over to me, placing a comforting hand on my shoulder. "Your biggest duty apart from the crown will be harboring the title of Potion's Master, alongside me."

NINETEEN

I send a dirty glare to the stack of weathered books on the table that are blocking my view of Chloe. "I'm never going to finish all of these!" With a huff, I bury my face in my hands.

Chloe's palm pushes the books out of the way. "You have all the time in the world. What's the rush?" she asks.

"I want to know everything now so that I can help Haven." I don't want to admit that I feel useless here. Everyone has been so welcoming, and Haven feels like home more than I can explain, but what do I have to offer them? I'll be queen, and I don't even know where to start with anything.

"I can help!" Mia sings, sipping a cup of tea at Chloe's little table.

I love Chloe's cottage. It's inviting, but I miss Alexander. He's been busy all day with something, I just don't know what.

"That's sweet, Mia, but I need to prepare you for school." I tell her.

She slouches, groaning. "Why do I have to go to school? I thought we were done with all that."

I snicker at her. "Education is important, and from what Chloe's told me, you're going to love this school." Her eyes widen in anticipation when Chloe begins to hum a melody. "Especially their music program." I tell her.

"Really! There's music here?" She almost bursts from her seat.

Chloe showcases her melodic voice with a short, unfamiliar, but beautiful song. She bows and we clap our hands with a smile. "We have very talented musicians of all kinds. No cello players, though, so they're excited for you to join."

"So, I'll be the odd one?" Mia groans.

Chloe gasps, feigning shock. "The odd one? Are you kidding! Every kid in Haven is dying to meet you. They haven't had a new kid since, well, ever!"

Mia smiles, but it doesn't reach her eyes. "I didn't have many friends at my old school, are you sure they'll like me?"

I place a hand on her arm. "They're going to love you, Mia. And if they don't, they'll have to deal with me."

I joke, earning a giggle from her. I turn my attention to Chloe, mulling over the list that makes no sense to me. "What does she need?"

"A shopping day! We'll go to the market downtown for supplies." She claps.

"Alexander told me to stay put until he gets back from whatever he's doing." I huff, frustrated that he wouldn't let me tag along this morning.

Chloe's attitude is carefree; she laughs and grabs her bag. "What he doesn't know won't hurt him." She touches her chin in thought. "But with you going in public, we may need to change your clothes, just in case."

I pull on my shirt and gesture to my jeans. "What's wrong with this?"

"So, so many things." she croaks.

"I want a pretty dress!" Mia chimes.

"Your wish is my command." Chloe says, flicking her wrist. Pink swirls escape from her fingers, encasing me and Mia. When the swirls clear the air, Mia's blonde hair is curled and she's swirling around in a pink dress.

"So pretty!" I sing. I'll never get over Chloe's talents. I look down and admire the long lavender gown I'm now wearing. It's not formal, which I feel more comfortable in, but it's still very pretty.

"Okay, I love this." I gush, touching the flowy fabric.

"I knew you would. Let's go!" she replies, shooing

us outside before I can change my mind.

"Will we change back at midnight?" Mia snickers and Chloe raises a brow. I try to explain to her and she finally agrees to read our storybooks.

The streets are bustling with life, and vendors spread out as far as the eye can see along the cobblestone path. "This is beautiful." I murmur in awe. The landscape around me is vibrant in color and music. Melodies play throughout the busy street, and there's a band nearby.

"You were right. They love music here!" Mia cries happily, her eyes widening with every step closer to the thrumming instruments.

All I can focus on are the people watching us and the smiles on their faces. "Everyone is staring at us." I whisper to Chloe, who smiles back at me.

"You're their princess. Just wave back and you'll be fine." she chimes.

I wave to the people, who seem genuinely excited to be around me. It's all so nice, but still out of my comfort zone. I don't like being the center of attention, and right now, that's exactly what I am.

Upon mulling over my decision to come here while Chloe was dragging us out of her cabin, I decided to bring a guard with us. Alexander seemed so adamant about me staying either inside the castle, or at Chloe's today, so maybe he'll be less mad when he surely finds out I did nothing that he asked since we have a guard for protection.

Chloe hums, stopping in front of a shop. The sign above the door reads, 'Mr. Albertsons' on an old, metal plaque.

"What do we get here?" I ask, clenching onto the list so I won't miss any of Mia's school supplies.

"While Mia doesn't have any magical abilities, her classmates do." Chloe ruffles Mia's hair. "And just like your sister, you'll be learning potions." she tells her.

"Ari, I can help!" Mia beams.

We walk inside the shop and the first thing I notice is a leather box on the counter, the top overflowing with wooden wands. A frail old man with a silver beard that falls to his stomach sits on a wooden chair, his eyes bright when he sees us. "Chloe, Princess Arianna, Mia." He bows his head.

"Hello!" Mia rushes up to him. "How do you know my name?"

His laugh is deep and full of joy. "I know a lot of things, like how you'll be starting at Haven's Academy this week."

I offer the man a smile. "She's a little nervous." I tell him, ignoring her when she groans in embarrassment.

He grips the handles of his chair and pushes himself up slowly before closing his hands around Mia's. "No need to be nervous, young lady. I went there, as well as everyone you see around you here. It's a wonderful place, full of magic and mystery." When he unclasps his hands, a purple caterpillar sits on her knuckles.

"I love caterpillars!" she yells while gently bringing her finger to touch the wiggly creature. He winks at us, and all worries leave my mind. We're in good hands in Haven; everyone here genuinely cares about us.

Walking around and collecting the things on Mia's list, I had almost forgotten the guard was with us until he appears next to me. "Miss, we have two more stops before going back to the castle."

Chloe grabs the list from my hand. "Let's get a move on then!" She smiles. The guard proceeds to pay for the contents of my basket, carrying the bags for us.

We walk through the different shops, meeting the people of Haven and gathering Mia's supplies.

I have to admit, I'm pretty jealous that I never attended a school filled with magic. I grab her list back from Chloe to tell Mia about her new schedule. "So, you'll have potions in the morning, intro to magic in the afternoon, and music class last."

"I'm so excited! But why intro to magic?" she wonders.

I don't know how to answer her, so I look to Chloe. "She'll be learning how—"

"Someone, help!" a desperate plea rings through my ears from afar, and I rush to it without hesitation. I struggle to maintain my balance as I attempt to squeeze through the townspeople who've crowded around the scene.

A woman around my age is knelt to the ground, clutching the hand of a little girl who lays on the cobblestone street.

The woman's eyes roam for help, but I can't quite see what happened through the crowd. "I need to get to her!" I shout, but no one can hear me over the chatter.

The guard, standing six-foot-tall and covered in metal, gets everyone's attention with the boisterous roar of his voice. "Make way for the princess!" he shouts.

The crowd easily parts and everything stills around us. The woman's eyes lock on mine, and her short brown hair moves along with the shake of her head. Chloe sighs beside me.

"Shit." she mutters upon seeing the woman's face.

"Anyone but her." The unfamiliar woman sneers as we approach.

I'm confused and concerned. "What does that mean?" I whisper to Chloe, who waves it off.

"I'll help her." Chloe offers. "Go back to the castle with the guard."

I ignore Chloe's help and advance to where the girl lays. I kneel down to assess the situation, my hands traveling to the place the girl points to. It looks twisted, but I can't be sure.

"It may be broken." I tell the woman.

She cuts her eyes to me, seething. "I said, we don't need *your* help."

The girl cries, clenching onto her leg. "Please, Leah. It hurts."

For whatever reason, Leah doesn't like me. But the moment a tear trickles down the girl's chin, she moves away to let me through.

"What's your name?" I ask the girl.

She wipes a few stray tears from her cheek. "It's Alice."

"Okay, Alice. What happened?" I distract her with questions while I take a closer look at her ankle.

"I got excited about getting my first wand and tripped on these stupid, uneven stones!" She smashes her tiny fist against the worn rocks and pulls back in pain.

"Let's not break anything else, okay?" I give her a smile, and she returns it. Alice has a warmth to her, unlike her sister. Maybe she was a bit traumatized seeing her sister fall, so she's lashing out? "My name is Arianna. Would you like to go to the castle with me? We will get you fixed right up!" My tone is light and airy.

Leah steps forward, holding out her hand to Alice. "That won't be necessary. I'll take her to Willow."

I shake my head. "Willow is busy today, preparing for classes to start. I'm all you've got." I tell her, unable to understand her apparent hatred for me. I ignore her attitude and instead focus on caring for Alice.

"Cloud!" I yell out, knowing he will always be there when I need him. A few moments later, the galloping feet of my majestic unicorn sounds throughout the busy street. "Alright, Alice. You ready to go?" I ask her.

"A unicorn!" She beams. The guard picks her up and places her on Cloud's back. "I've never seen one so close!" She's so excited, but you can tell in her voice that she's in pain.

The moment I go to climb on Cloud, Leah holds out her hands to her sister. "I'll take you there myself." she chides.

"This will be much faster." I assure her.

Chloe shakes her head, telling me to not push it. "Let's just go, Ari. We can meet them there."

I hold my ground, unable to let her walk. "No. I'm a nurse. It's my obligation to help. Let me help."

"Ari," Chloe pleads as the crowd around us dissipates.

Leah steps directly in front of me. "Get out of my way." she snaps.

I consider just letting Leah ride to the castle with her sister, but I'm worried she'll head straight to Willow's shop and no one will be there. "May I ask what your problem is?"

She rolls her eyes, gesturing to me. "You, Arianna Castelle, are my problem."

I shake my head, confused. "I don't even know

you."

   She scoffs, as if I'm supposed to understand her hatred for me. "You ruined my life."

TWENTY

With Leah being extremely adamant about Alice not going anywhere with me, I ride to the castle on Cloud's back with Mia. Chloe sits on my shoulder in fairy form.

"I don't understand what would make her hate me so much that she would take her sister, who is in pain, on a longer route to get help." I throw my head back, angered by the situation.

"Well ..." Chloe begins hesitantly.

"What?" I ask, not liking her lingering sentence.

"She was kind of ... Alexander's girlfriend." she admits.

Before I can respond, we reach the castle gates. Alexander stands with his arms crossed looking dangerously handsome and incredibly irritated.

As he helps me off of Cloud, his blue eyes bore into me. "Care to explain to me why you were walking around town all day?"

I give him a sheepish look. "How did you know?" I ask.

"A future princess mulling around Haven is hot gossip, Ms. Castelle." He kisses my cheek. "You look beautiful."

"Thank you," I blush, turning my face away for a moment. "Why did you want me to stay here? I thought you said we were safe."

"Of course you're safe. But not everyone is good, Arianna. You need a personal guard." he tells me.

"We brought one!" I sing.

Alexander looks around before lifting my arm and Mia's hair, which makes her giggle. "Where is he?"

I roll my eyes, laughing. "He's coming. A girl got hurt and she's on the way here."

He instantly grows concerned, his eyes hovering over my body. "What happened? Are you okay?"

He checks on Mia, who clutches her big stack of books. "I'm fine! A girl broke her leg, I think." Mia says.

"Ankle." I correct.

Alexander nods, looking behind us. "Where is she?"

I place my hands on my hips, "Her delightful sister wouldn't let her come here with me, but they're on the way." I don't elaborate further. I've never really had a boyfriend; only a few flings here and there, but never anything serious. Although Alexander was only in my dreams, it was always enough for me.

I'm not accustomed to the seething jealously that's steadily coursing through my veins. "Who was it?" he asks, crossing his arms.

Chloe shakes her head. "You're not going to be happy." she tells him.

She doesn't need to elaborate further; I can tell by the annoyance on his face that he knows exactly who we're talking about.

"Move!" Leah yells, announcing her grand arrival to the castle gates. She pushes her way through the guards and Alexander sighs.

He looks to me, running a hand through his thick, dark hair. "I'm so sorry, Ari."

I look away. "It's fine. Let's just fix Alice."

Alice wobbles next to her sister. She shouldn't be on her feet at all right now. "It still hurts!" she cries.

Leah's face is red; one can tell this is the last place she wants to be. "My magic only does so much, Alice. Sorry Willow wasn't at the shop to help you."

Alexander walks over and scoops Alice up, and she sends me a wave. "I don't mind the future princess fixing me." she swoons.

I appreciate her kindness, but I feel like it's making

Leah seethe further. We all head to the infirmary in silence. As Alexander carries Alice, Leah walks closely beside him, blocking my typical spot next to him.

"If she would have been paying attention to where she walked, I wouldn't be having to come here." she groans.

"Seems like it was an accident." Alexander replies.

Leah ignores him, waving her hand mindlessly. "Now I missed my hair appointment."

I must have mistaken what I thought was worry for her sister for selfishness. The more she babbles on about her missed appointment to an annoyed Alexander, the angrier I get.

We're both grown women. Why can't we be cordial to each other?

Once we arrive to the infirmary, I gesture to the cot. "Lay her here." I order Alexander. Chloe zooms around the room, collecting my things.

Alexander looks around, and his eyes roam over me. "Need anything, babe?"

"Some water would be nice." Leah answers with a cocky smirk.

I roll my eyes at her audacity, laughing when Alice does the same. "Some ice would be helpful, Alexander. Thank you."

Alice groans in pain when I clean the dirt around her foot and apply gauze to her ankle. "I'm sorry about her." she whispers, making sure to be quiet enough so Leah doesn't hear her.

I wave it off. "Don't apologize; it's not your fault. And good news! It's twisted, not broken." I wrap the gauze securely around her ankle.

"What about school?" She deflates, beginning to tear up.

"School won't go anywhere, and you'll need to stay off this foot for a few weeks. I'll get Chloe to make you some crutches and you'll be better in no time."

"Thank you, princess." Alice grins.

Leah looks annoyed as I guide her to the side to have a word about the care that Alice will need. "You'll need to ice it every two hours to keep the swelling down." I tell her, discreetly waving Alexander away when he begins to walk to us. I can deal with an angry ex on my own. Plus, if she thinks she can respond to him saying 'babe', there's going to be an issue that will need to be dealt with between us ladies.

She holds her hand up, her eyes roaming her manicured nails. "Can't you do that? I mean, that's what you're here for right?" She lazily looks to me, her head tilted. "The help."

I stand tall, not letting her words affect me outwardly. "Actually, I'm here to marry Alexander. As for your sister, she's welcome to stay in the castle and I can watch over her if you're not capable."

Leah scoffs, shaking her head. "You shouldn't be marrying him." She takes a menacing step toward me. "I should." she growls.

I quiet my breathing, not wanting to engage in this pointless conversation any further. "The gauze needs to stay taut on her ankle, if it gets wet it needs to be changed immediately. Chloe's going to ma—"

Leah leans in close, cutting me off. "Listen, girl," she hisses, her tone at a calculated whisper. "That crown was mine. You don't deserve it."

I shake my head in disbelief. "Alexander is mine, and I do deserve him." I reply in a very cordial, level tone.

"Everything okay over here?" Alexander arrives, slinking his arm around my back and holding me tightly to him.

With a flourish, Leah turns on her heels and marches towards her sister. "Get up. It's time to leave."

"Wait! I need the crutches." Alice tells her.

Chloe stumbles in with Mia close behind. "They're finished!"

"They have glitter!" Alice gleams.

Chloe points to Mia. "That was her idea." She winks.

Alice's eyes widen. "You're the new girl, Mia!" she says excitedly.

Mia extends her hand and Alice takes it. "Hi, I'm Mia."

"Alice!" she sings. "I'll be the one showing you around Haven Academy tomorrow!" As soon as Alice finishes her sentence, she frowns. "Or maybe not, since I'm hurt."

"That's okay! We can hang out at the castle after school, if you'd like?" Mia suggests, and before she can answer, Leah rushes her sister out the door of the infirmary.

"Don't worry. When we get home, I'll accelerate the healing so you'll be better way quicker." She turns to look at me one last time. "Some of us are more useful than others." Her insidious gaze turns to Alexander. "Let me know when you get bored of her."

Alexander's jaw sets at her words. "That will never happen."

I wind down from the day's events with a glass of sweet red wine on the balcony and sulk in the unusual sting of jealousy.

"I'm sorry about that." Alexander says, walking up beside me and placing his hand on my shoulder. I ignore his freshly showered scent and the way he has no shirt on. When I don't respond, he frowns. "Don't listen to her babe. She wouldn't be able to accelerate anything if you didn't begin the healing process yourself." he tells me, assuming I'm upset about the other comments and not about how she is obsessed with him or how inadequate it makes me feel to know they probably ...

"It's fine. I just didn't know you were already taken." I reply stiffly.

His laugh travels through the area as he sits beside me. "No one has ever owned my heart but you."

I grit my teeth, not wanting to talk about this. "How many girls exactly have thought they had your heart?" I ask.

He scratches the nape of his neck, avoiding the question. When I nudge him, he finally answers. "The past doesn't matter." he says simply, avoiding the question.

"It does to me."

When he shakes his head, his thick, damp hair falls above his brows. "I see nothing but you, so please don't be jealous. There's no one else for me."

I smile. "I am a little jealous." And ashamed to admit it. "I'm just kind of worried." I flush.

"Of what?" he wonders, cocking his head curiously.

I twirl the delicate glass stem in my hand, questions swirling in my mind matching the whirling of wine. "It's just that you've been with someone before," He tilts his head and looks away. "Multiple people." I add, huffing. "And I'm ... ya know?"

"You're what?" he gives me an incredulous look.

I throw my head back. "I've done things with other men." I admit, and he tenses, a pang of jealousy rippling over him that's more than a little obvious. "But not ... that." I breathe out and watch as his stiff muscles relax at my confession.

He nods his head, taking the tips of his fingers and running them along my exposed neckline. "Don't worry. I'll take good care of you."

"But what if I'm not good? What if you wished you were with—"

He swoops down, stopping my words with a heated kiss. His soft lips trail to my neck where he peppers kisses along my skin until finally, he whispers deeply into my ear. "There's no one in this world or yours that I would want to ravish in bed more than I do you, Arianna."

My cheeks heat at his words. I turn away and bring the sweet wine back to my lips.

"What have you been doing all day?" I blush, changing the subject.

He laughs at my change of conversation. "Preparing something for you."

When I tilt my head in inquiry, he stands and extends his hand to me. "Follow me and I'll show you." he answers a question I didn't ask, but one he knew from my expression. I love how well we can read each other. He helps me up and I don't miss the sultry look that beams in his eyes.

I giggle as he blindfolds me outside of the castle gates. "Where are we going?" I squeal, fueled with excitement.

"You'll know soon, my love." He whispers against my neck, and a tingling sensation covers my body filling my needy skin with prickled chills.

We walk for a few moments, the ground beneath my feet changing every so often. Soft, hard, crunchy, sandy. "I can hear the ocean." I say, inhaling the healing, salty air that surrounds us, air that wraps us both in a warm embrace.

A few feet in front of me, I feel the crunch of dry leaves under my shoes. The ocean being next to a forest tells me exactly where we are. "We're at our own Haven." I grin.

"You're too smart for your own good. Don't take off that blindfold until I instruct, alright?" he gently orders.

I nod, continuing through the dense woods and loving this playful side of him. A crackling fire is near, and a moment later, Alexander's hands are on my bare shoulders. The only thing between us is a thin, short dress.

"We're here." He whispers hotly into my ear.

My hands rise to remove the cloth that cover my vision, but he stops me. "I didn't tell you to take it off." Alexander growls lightly, his fingers sliding under the strap of my dress.

I take in a deep breath as his finger toys with the fabric covering my body. "I want to see you, all of you." he says gruffly. My heart pounds from anticipation. With my sight gone, all other senses are heightened. The sounds of animals chirping is calming, the crackling fire is romantic and produces a woodsy smell, and Alexander's touch is inviting and sensual.

"Kiss me." I beg softly.

His hands explore my exposed skin, and he grunts when my dress falls to a heap at his feet.

I gasp when I'm softly pushed against the trunk of a tree, my back protected by one of his large hands. His breath is heavy and full of lust. "You are breathtaking." Alexander whispers. His body is pressed against mine, and fire swarms between us. His thick, hard length pulses against my bare leg.

Slowly, his fingertips glide over my stomach until they reach the top of my panties. Nerves kick in when I realize how exposed I am without being able to see. "What if someone sees us?" I moan, unfamiliar with the sultry tone of my voice.

His firm grip travels over the length of my body, and he squeezes every place that makes me squirm. "I would never fucking *ever* let anyone see you like this."

"Alexander," I moan when his finger glides between my legs. I know he can feel the dampness through my silk panties.

"Arianna," he says my name slowly, deliberately. His tongue swipes my neck, then my lips, the force parting them. I beg to see him doing this, but he refuses to lift the blindfold.

In a heated frenzy, we collide. I'm not surprised by his strength when he picks me up with ease, wrapping my legs around his waist as we travel closer to the roaring fire.

He lays me down on my back against a soft blanket, his body traveling down mine. Further, and further. His fingertips wrap around the top of my panties, and I lift my hips to help him remove them.

I hear the small thud they make when they land on far off leaves.

"I can't wait to taste you." Alexander groans. His tongue flicks against my throbbing clit and a heady moan escapes my lips. "Fuck." he hisses, his tongue working magic on me while his hands greedily grip my breasts. "Remove it."

The moment the blindfold slips from my grip, I gasp in pleasure.

It was already a euphoric feeling when I couldn't see him, but now with the way his eyes are locked on mine it's extremely intimate.

The way he's positioned between my legs, peering at me with his bright blue eyes through thick black lashes. The sensual way his tongue is lapping me while his muscles constrict from the control he's trying so desperately to maintain. Every moment of this is so, so erotic.

"It's ..." I can't stop the moans that escape me. My head falls back from pleasure while his tongue searches my body. "Perfect." I tell him. The ambience makes everything more intense. A roaring fire ignites beside me, and specks of embers float above to the starry sky peeking through the trees. The moonlight and fire encase us in a romantic glow.

He lifts his head up for a moment, his eyes glossed over.

"You like what I do to you?" His tone is deeper than usual, more earthy. When I nod, his hands grip both of my legs firmly as he holds them apart. I'm not trying to close them, but the pressure of his hands pressing against my skin is titillating.

As his tongue discovers me, he takes his thumb and rubs small circles on my clit, sending my body into a shaking frenzy.

My head dives back along with my eyes as they roll in the back of my head. The roaring campfire ignites more heat against my already scorching skin as I discover the most earth-shattering orgasm.

I collapse within myself, breathing heavily and still wanting more from him. I look back down to find my fingers are trapping Alexander's thick, dark hair. He looks up to me, licking his lips. "Delicious." he tells me, making me wither at his words.

His massive frame slides on top of me, engulfing me. He kisses over and over along my flushed cheeks. "This is beautiful, Alexander."

"I've been preparing it for you all day. The cabin

may be burned down, but I couldn't wait another second to take you. We're staying here in that tent." He nudges his head to the side.

The butterflies in my stomach dance, and my mind whirls with anticipation. "I love you." I tell him, but it doesn't feel like a big enough sentence to describe my feelings.

"I love you more than my dreams would ever allow, Arianna." Alexander replies, and I smile; that saying makes more sense for us.

The twinkling lights from above cast a golden hue against his tan skin as he stands, and when he takes off his shirt, light gleams against his toned body. I clench my legs, unable to wait any longer.

The sounds of nature fill the air, and my body excites further at the sound of his zipper flying down and the soft thud of his pants hitting the dirt. My breath hitches when he bends down on the blanket, bulging from his boxers.

He slides them off, and I gasp at the size.

"Um—I—" I don't know how to word my sentence, because I'm worried, but his hand travels through my hair reassuringly.

"Don't worry." He kisses me gently. He slides in between my open legs, the tip of him pressing against me. "I'll never hurt you, Arianna." His eyes are dark and full of want.

A build of pressure tingles every nerve ending in my body as he slides into me.

My head rolls back in pleasure, with a slight tinge of uncomfortableness from his size but he takes his time. Alexander rolls his hips slowly and rocks into me at a perfect pace while my body becomes accustomed to him.

"You feel like home." he moans, and his deep euphoric words make me squirm.

"You feel ... huge." I give him a wry smile and laugh, unsure how else to describe the fullness I feel.

He chuckles too, but it's deep and matches the darkness surrounding us. I run my hand through his tousled hair as he sinks further into me, devouring me with his body. "Are you okay?" he asks while gritting his teeth. I know he's using every bit of patience to do this slow and steady.

"Mhmm," I reply, my lips barely parted. Alexander makes sure to touch every single inch of my body as I grow more and more used to his length. I moan when his teeth graze my hard nipples.

He thrusts harder, and the uncomfortable feeling has turned into a euphoric rhythm. With each thrust, I moan his name into the night air.

He tilts his head, his malachite necklace dangling in front of my face. "You feel heavenly wrapped around me. Just look at you! Perfection," He kisses my cheek as he pounds into me, uncontrolled and wild.

I love it.

He continues to talk, and it sends me closer to the edge again. "The way your heated skin matches your crimson hair, I want to make you feel this way every second."

"Don't stop." I plead, unsure I ever want this feeling to go away. Skin to skin, his warmth radiating over my body, our eyes locked on one another.

"Arianna,"

"Y—Yes?"

He slows his pace, his eyes watching my face carefully, expectantly. "Marry me."

TWENTY-ONE

We're in a heap on the soft blanket, tangled together under the stars after an unforgettable moment together. Alexander is in only his uniform pants, me in one of his t-shirts and a pair of boxers.

"That was incredible." he says, twirling my hair between his long fingers.

Nerves creep in, sinking their teeth into this blissful moment and making me worry I didn't do enough. "It was amazing for me, but you don't have to lie. I wasn't—"

His hands grip my face, and he lands a passionate kiss on my lips. "Don't ever let any such nonsense come from those perfect lips again. This is the best night I've ever had."

I blush, thankful for the night sky's darkness hiding my cheeks. "I can't believe you did all of this for me." I gesture to the twinkling lights, the roaring fire, the wine and cheese.

"I wanted it to be special." He shrugs.

I nod, unable to control my grin. "It was perfect."

He looks up, laying on his back. "Did you mean what you said?"

"Of course." I tell him.

Alexander grins, sitting up and turning towards me. "I vow to honor you, protect you, and defend your name for the rest of my life, Arianna. I'm the luckiest man in Haven to have a bride like you."

As he seals his promises with a kiss, he slides a ring onto my finger.

The light catches on the shimmering stone. "It's gorgeous!" I squeal, admiring the simple yet intricate detail of the ring.

His fingertip grazes against it. "I designed it, but Chloe brought it to life."

"Of course she did. She's amazing." I gaze at the ring, taking in the thin golden band with Alexander's family crest embedded in replacement of the usual worldly diamond.

"The stone in the crest is aba—" he begins before I cut him off.

"Abalone, the stone of the heart." I finish his sentence, beaming.

"You've been reading the books Willow gave you." He nods his head appreciatively.

I shake my head, confused. "No, I haven't even started. I know all kinds of herbs, remedies, and healing stones from my world, but I'm not sure why I knew what this was." I look to my hand curiously.

Alexander shrugs, happily pulling a vial from a basket and taking a swig. He hands the contents to me.

"What is it?"

"Tradition," He grins. "Just drink."

The liquid slides down my throat, leaving a faint hint of orange behind. "I don't feel anything. Is it liquor?"

"No, it's the same stuff I gave Mason. Truth serum."

A small gasp escapes me. "Why?"

His tone is casual. "It's custom before a wedding for the bride and groom to do this ritual in order to show each other that their feelings are true."

"What about trust?" I frown.

He laughs, trailing his hands up my leg. "It's just an old tradition. There's nothing to worry about." He sits up, animated with his hands. "Ask me anything."

"Okay, um," I think for a moment. "What do you want most right this second?" I ask, twirling my fingertips through his hand.

"To be inside you again." Alexander laughs.

"Oh," I turn away from his bluntness, worried what truths I might reveal with my eyes.

"And what's your deepest desire?" he asks.

"To be with you forever." I tell him, immediately clamping my hand over my mouth. I had no power over the words that came out. Even though it was true, the feeling of loss of control was odd. "How is this working here? I thought no magic was allowed?"

"Chloe put up a new barrier spell but tweaked it a little for emergencies." He looks away, remembering the horrible day his father was hurt. "We can't risk anyone getting hurt again, so potions and healing like you do are allowed."

A still silence passes through when he nudges me to go. I don't want to embarrass myself with the questions that wander through my mind.

His eyes bore into mine. "This is a night where you can ask me anything you desire, Arianna. Without judgement," He leans over and grabs the cheese board, setting it beside us.

Before I can stop myself, I spit it out. "Do you still love Leah?"

"I never loved her." he replies immediately.

I nod. "Do you ever miss her?"

"No." he responds, unflinching. I take in a deep breath, laughing at myself for considering that he would love someone so vile.

"My turn." He grins, his eyes gleaming against the crackling fire. "Those men you spoke of earlier." His jaw clenches. "Have you ever been in love?"

"Only with you." I reply.

"I don't like the thought of other men around

you." he admits, his eyes growing dark. "It doesn't sit right with me, but all of that's in the past. I own your heart now."

"You do." I smile, knowing I'm not alone on the jealousy train.

He nods his head in my direction, and I dive into the harder questions that have been weighing on my mind. "Do you want to be king?" I wonder, twirling a grape in my fingers.

He grits his teeth, trying not to answer. "No." He shakes his head; one can tell this is something he doesn't want to admit. "My place is to defend, to fight. If I became king, I wouldn't be allowed to battle."

I recall everyone's talks of safety and security. "Is there anyone to fight?"

"People will lie; they'll tell you Haven is perfect, and for the most part it is. But there's magic, and where there's light, darkness is lurking behind." There's a sharp intake of breath. "I am the darkness now, Arianna. But I refuse to let it consume me. There are still battles to be fought, rouges, traitors, monsters." I look warily around the dark woods. "Not here. I would know if someone was here." He lifts his wrist, showcasing a small bracelet with a tiny blue pendant.

"What is it?" I ask.

"I'm not taking any chances after, Mason. Chloe also implemented a little security system. This is a tracker. If anyone steps on our land, it lights up. Now, it's my turn."

he says, a mischievous grin spreading across his face. "What are you thinking about?"

"You, naked." I groan, mad at my brain.

He laughs, sliding closer to me on the blanket.

TWENTY-TWO

It's been a week since Alexander proposed, and I happily accepted. The castle has been in a frenzy ever since, preparing for the wedding.

Today, I broke away to help Willow on her day off from teaching.

A bell rings when I kick open the door to the shop. "Willow?" I call out, closing the door behind me and almost dropping the small pallet of herbs she asked me to bring from the castle garden.

"Arianna!" she calls out happily. I follow her voice to a back-storage room. "Over here, dear. Just place it on the far corner of that shelf." Willow says, gesturing to a small clearing on one of the stocked shelves.

When I've come by to work this week, I've been too busy burying my head in one particular book to notice much of anything else.

I walk over, setting the dried herbs down amidst the familiar dust of her shop and stepping back to admire the amount of vials in this room. "How many potions do you have?" I ask.

Willow stands up, dusting off her apron. "Oh, Haven! Hundreds, maybe thousands!" she replies.

I nod, running my hands over some of the glasses. "Where do you keep your poisons?" I shrug my shoulders and attempt to make this sound like a normal question.

Willow laughs, shaking her head. "You've been buried in the poison book all week. I'm glad you finally asked me about it so I don't start to worry that you've gone mad." She grins.

I walk over to her as she pulls a wooden box from the top shelf. "There's something I want to create," I tell her, dusting off the top of the old box with my palm.

She coughs when the dust speckles settle. "I can help, but this stuff is very dangerous."

I nod; reading over the book of poisons and potions all week made me shiver from fear at what some of them can do.

Willow retreats to grab that book, returning with it and a rolling tray lined with glass beakers and bottles. "So, what is it you need all this for?" she asks, pulling on a pair of gloves and handing me a set.

I pull them down tight against my fingers, hoping

my plan works. "There's a man who tests our food."

"Ah," Willow acknowledges. "And you don't want him to die?"

I nod. "Correct. I think he's paid for his crimes enough, and while I may not be fit to be a queen or princess, I can help with things like this."

Willow's eyes roam over me, a small laugh escaping her, but she doesn't say anything further.

I flip through my notes. "So, what I've found is that nearly every poison here has an anchor. A chemical compound that corresponds with one another." I say.

Willow's eyes excitedly look over the countless notes I've taken. "You want to create a detector?" she asks.

"Yes!" I grin. "I'm thinking of a powder—tasteless, of course. One that can be poured on our food and into our drinks that will change colors upon contact with a deadly substance."

A low whistle escapes her lips. "Genius." She smiles.

"Can we do it?" I ask.

Willow pulls down her glasses, getting ready for work. "We can most certainly try."

Hours pass as we work in steady motions to create a powdered elixir that can change the fate of Haven's prisoners while simultaneously keeping people safe beyond that.

"Just one more drop." I say, focused entirely on not spilling the essence of hemlock into the closed area we're in.

I look to Willow, waiting for her to show me a sign that we've done it. "Now to poison our food." she giggles, taking the deadliest potion ever created, made by us, and pouring it over a slice of apple pie along with a cup of tea. I then scoop out the powder we created, sprinkling it over the plate of pie along with a dash in the cup. The powder responds, turning into a bright purple to indicate danger.

"I'll do more testing over the week, but I think it's safe to say Alfie is free to go." Willow sings.

It's my first task, above many more, but I'm proud of myself for seeing it through. Now a man who stole bread for his family won't die from tasting our lunch. I don't mean to be judgmental of the punishments chosen by Haven for their prisoners, I just think this is a better way.

"Thank you for all your help." I tell her, reeling from what we did and the success of our experiment.

"Of course, dear." she replies. "Oh, and Arianna. About what you said of not being fit for queen?" Her eyes roam my face, a look of happiness in them. "You were wrong. You're spending your wedding week not gushing over flowers or worrying over dresses, but instead focusing on this alone. It's admirable and you are more than fit to bear the crown."

I blush, wondering if she's right. "Thank you." I say, wrapping my arms around her in a tight hug. "It means so much to have your help." When I pull back, I wipe a tear from my cheek, and we head into the main shop area.

I put away my things, happy I'll be able to start on the books I need to become Potion's Master this week. "What got you interested in all of this?" I ask, admiring Willow's collection of potions.

She flashes a warm smile, the kind that tells me to take a seat while she dives into her past. "When I was a little girl, around Mia's age, I had an older sister." Willow says, looking away with tears welling in her eyes.

"You don't have to continue." I assure her, not knowing that it was a sad subject.

"No, it's okay. It's nice to talk about her." She smiles fondly, but her eyes are sad. "We thought we were invincible, like nothing could touch us."

A few moments pass. "Did something happen to her?" I ask.

"We were in the forest, drawing energy from the large mushrooms you see out there. Casting spells like little witches do when they're up to no good," She lets out a chuckle.

My brow quirks. "Wait, you're a witch?"

Willow grins. "I haven't practiced in decades." She looks into the distance. "We did a spell, it was dark ..." Her smile grows somber again.

"Black magic." I breathe, only hearing about it in stories.

"Indeed." she replies, grabbing a nearby photo album. She flips to a page and points to a young girl, about fifteen, standing beside her.

"It's animated!" I say with surprise.

"Yes, it's enchanted. Stealing a moment in time, forever encased in a book." Her finger grazes the moving photo and a beat of silence passes through the quiet shop. Finally, she speaks again. "Her name was Blossom." Was? I watch the way Willow smiles at the old photo, not being able to imagine her loss. If something ever happened to Mia, I don't know what I would do.

"The dark magic invaded her body and destroyed her from the inside until she was nothing but ash." Tears trickle down her cheeks and I hug her again. Fear courses through me at the correlation to Alexander's darkness that swirls inside of him.

But it's not black magic, it's darkness … right?

If I ask Willow, it will worry her, but I need to talk to him tonight.

"I don't practice magic anymore, but I wanted to help Haven, so I turned to nature and became a Potion's Master." She grabs a napkin, dabbing tears from her rosy cheeks. "Which is something you'll never be if you don't start reading those other books." Willow teases, but I know she's right.

The tense moment is washed away with our laughter. Learning more about Willow helps me to understand her more, and I'm thankful she shared it with me.

She looks up and takes in a deep, refreshing breath. "Onto more positive matters!" She smiles. "Are you ready for your wedding tomorrow?"

I beam, unable to hold back my excitement. "Yes! It's going to be amazing, but I worry about the ceremony. From what I've heard, it's much different from where I come from."

Willow smiles, placing her cool hand on my cheek. "You'll do just fine, dear. It's not as scary as they make it seem."

My eyes pan to her hand, where a golden band sits. "How was your wedding?" I ask.

Quickly, she looks away. "That was many moons ago, darling."

"Anyone I know?" I wonder, having gotten to know the people of Haven in the short time I've been here and never noticing Willow with a husband.

She looks away, that lost look returning to her face. "Lost love happens. It's not something we should talk about now, too depressing."

I frown, trapping her hand in mine. "Willow, you and Chloe are my closest friends. If you need to talk about anything, I'm here for you."

"Thank you, Arianna." She dusts off her hands. "But the past is done, and we can only look towards the future."

I stand, starting to organize the nearby potions and focusing on less heavy conversations to not upset Willow; she'll open up when she's ready. I notice a unique bottle on the shelf in the shape of a heart with a cork embedded in it. "This one's pretty." I say.

"Go ahead and tuck that in your pocket. You can thank me later," She winks.

"What's it for?" I inquire.

"Your wedding night. It's a powerful love potion. Advanced enough to intensify, well," She flushes crimson. "Everything." Willow winks, gesturing for me to take it. I slip the small vial into my pocket. "That should be all for today. Don't you need to head to the castle and prepare?"

"Yes!" Chloe sings, bursting through the doors and pointing an accusatory finger at me.

"Oh no," I croak.

"He told me you would be here!" Her face is scrunched, and I try to hold back laughter. "I didn't believe him. Tomorrow is your wedding day, young lady!" she howls.

I cross my arms, grinning from her use of the word. "Young lady?" I say, arching a brow.

"I'm centuries older than you and with no patience to boot. You're coming with me!" she happily demands.

Willow walks forward, shaking her head. "Oh, I know what this is." She grins.

"What?" I ask, looking between the two of them.

Aurora swoops in behind Chloe, and I notice how dressed up they are. "It's party time." Aurora claps her hands.

I don't see any tiny people with them. "Wait! Where's Mia?" I ask.

Chloe throws her hands up, waving it off. "She's with Douglas making him have a tea party."

I turn to Willow to see if she'd like to come, but she's already walking into the back office. "Where are we going?" I dare to ask.

Chloe fluffs my hair, winking. "To get wasted!"

TWENTY-THREE

The bright sun burns as it bursts through the window, illuminating the bedroom. I squeeze my eyes shut, gripping my throbbing head. "Oh, my god. What happened last night?" I croak.

Chloe shoots up from the bed, her pink hair a matted mess. "You drank the entire bottle of Troll's feet." she replies.

"Eww!" I cringe, sticking my tongue out.

"It's not a real troll." Aurora sweeps across the room, bright-eyed and ready for the day. "It's just a strong liquor they drink. Now, get up! We have so much to do."

She flings open the curtains, allowing more pain-inducing light to seep into the cottage. "Ugh, close it!" Chloe demands.

"Just another hour of sleep, please." I plead with

Aurora.

"Okay, so you want to show up to your wedding twenty minutes late?" she replies, shrugging. "Fine by me."

I shoot up from the couch, Chloe rushes into the kitchen. "Cloud didn't wake us up! He was supposed to neigh at the door hours ago!" She stomps her foot.

I lazily plop off the couch. "Is he okay?" I ask, walking out the front door and finding him snoozing on the grass.

When I walk back in, Aurora shrugs. "We had him out all night. He was tired."

I run a hand over my face. This can't be happening. "Where's Mia?"

"I've already been to the castle. She's fine; Douglas is bringing her here. But you need to get ready, pronto!" Aurora says.

She is usually the calm one, but today she's a ball of energy. "Did we at least have enough fun to explain the pain I'm in?" I ask, gripping my head and trying to calm my pounding headache.

"I took pictures!" Aurora sings, rushing over and handing me a stack of moving photos.

"I danced on a table?" I groan, worried about what kind of impression that made on the people of Haven. I have to hold myself to a higher standard. "How many people saw that?" I wonder.

"That's why we went to the troll's den." Aurora

assures me. "First time trolls and fairies have done that in centuries." She grins.

Chloe takes the images from my hands. "Ew, I kissed Krempan!" She sticks her tongue out in disgust.

"Not just Krempan." Aurora laughs and we all burst into a fit of giggles, but our pounding headaches send us almost hurling over the toilet a few doors down.

Willow bursts through the doors holding a small basket. "I'm here, ladies!"

Chloe throws her head back. "Oh, thank Haven."

She hands us each a potion bottle, filled to the brim. "Drink up. We have to get going!"

The clear liquid zooms down my throat, instantly giving me relief. My mind is clear, and my body feels rested. "Hangover elixir?" I ask, baffled.

"It's more for sickness, but I've found it works for both." She winks. I would know this if I would have started on my untouched stack of books.

Calming down, I stretch my stiff muscles. "Are you nervous?" Willow asks.

I shake my head. "Not at all. Excited, actually! Maybe the tiniest bit nervous about the ceremony, though." I admit.

Willow places a calming hand on me. "I told you yesterday, you'll do great."

Chloe is excited and wired as usual. "Okay, what do you want your dress to look like?" She asks with wild eyes.

Without hesitation, I tell her. "Surprise me."

She almost chokes on her tea. "On your wedding day?"

I shrug, placing my faith in her without worry. "I trust you; you'll design the most perfect dress. Go crazy." I tell her.

She snickers while bringing her fingertips to the air, her smile reaching her eyes.

Mid-transformation, Douglas and Mia waltz through the door. I go to cover myself, but Chloe has already placed a heavy robe over my dress. She squeals in delight, and I can't wait to see it.

"Umm, do you need anything dear? I'm about to head out the back." Willow whispers.

"The back?" I ask confused, worrying about the broken look behind her eyes.

Douglas is busy helping Mia set her stuff near the front door and Willow leans in close. "Remember what I said about lost love?" She nods her head forward.

"Douglas?" I whisper in shock.

"Shh!" she cries. "Please get me out of here—"

Douglas coughs, looking massive in the tiny cottage. "Willow..." he says her name slowly, hurt in his voice obvious as he gazes at her intently.

"Douglas," she replies, their eyes not leaving each other's. The room stands still for a moment before she peels her gaze from his and disappears quickly into the kitchen.

I can't help her or do anything more than stand still while Aurora and Chloe busy themselves around me, their hands running through my already styled hair.

Douglas approaches me, holding his hand out. "You look stunning, princess." He kisses the back of my hand before bowing.

"Please, call me Ari." I tell him, giggling at the fact that I'm in a heavy robe.

"Ari." He grins.

Chloe shoes him away. "No boys allowed; we have no time!" I've never seen her so flustered but still so in her element.

As Douglas exits, sheepishly looking back to Willow a few times as he does, Chloe turns her attention to Mia. "What color dress would you like, little princess?"

I shake my head. "Oh! I already know the colors of all your dresses."

"Ours?" Chloe and Aurora ask in unison.

I nod. "You too, Willow." I chime.

"Hmm?" She lifts her head from the cupboard, clearly still lost in thought.

I look to the ladies who have helped me feel welcome since my first moment of arrival in Haven. "Where I come from, we have bridesmaids. They help us get ready for the day."

"Odd, but I love it! What color?" Chloe asks.

"Lavender." I tell her.

Moments later, all the ladies are in floor-length lavender gowns, their hair all in perfect updos.

Chloe grabs my shoulders, peeling the heavy robe off. "Enough of us. It's your turn to see yourself!" she squeals.

Mia jumps up and down. "You look like a princess!"

Aurora nods her head with a smile. "That's because she is."

A tear falls down Willow's cheek. "Absolutely breathtaking,"

I blush from the attention and their compliments as I walk to the mirror with my eyes closed. Mia guides me by holding my hand.

I gasp when I see my reflection. A fitted bodice hugs my chest while lace lays out to form a long, bustling train that sweeps around the cottage floor.

It's not a ball gown like Cinderella; it's better. Like it was made specifically for me. I don't try to stop the tears that dance down my cheeks. My red hair is pulled up into an elegant updo, a few strands framing my face.

"Don't cry, dear. You'll ruin your makeup." Willow hands me a napkin and I dab it underneath my eyes before looking back to the three women and one girl who all have their hands under their chins with big smiles.

"It's so beautiful, Chloe." I croak, more emotional than I've ever been. "Is it time?" I ask.

"It is." Chloe nods.

Nerves rustle through me. "What will happen at the wedding? I don't want to screw this up," I desperately wish to see Alexander; he calms me.

"Me and Aurora will carry you down the aisle, and your feet won't touch the ground." she tells me, but that's what I was afraid of.

"Just you two? You're so tiny in fairy form."

"We may be tiny, but we're strong!" Both fairies show off their muscles, earning a laugh from Mia.

"What else?"

"You'll vow to each other your promises, and seal them with a kiss."

"Okay, that's familiar." I breathe easier.

Willow hands me a blade. "And then you will do the blood oath." she says simply, prompting a quick drop of my stomach.

"Blood oath!" I cry.

"Just kidding." She takes the blade and chuckles. "After the kiss, we celebrate!" We all burst into laughter.

My fears seemingly float away as we head outside, until I see the rows of the people of Haven lining the street. Douglas waits at the edge of the steps for me. "You waited?" I ask him, my heart pounding from all of the cheers.

"I wanted to accompany you, if you don't mind." He bows.

"I would love that." The gesture melts my heart. I always knew one day when I would get married that my dad, Frank, wouldn't be sober enough to walk in a straight line down the aisle, so an escort by Douglas, who has been so kind to me since my arrival, is more than I could have dreamed of.

Cloud neighs and my eyes pan to him. "Cloud! Look at you!" He's wearing a little tux with a bow tie around his neck.

"That was my idea." Mia exclaims with a swoon.

Behind Cloud is a golden carriage. Mia's eyes widen the closer we get to it.

Douglas holds his arm out. "Shall we?" he asks. As we near the carriage, he opens the door and Mia jumps inside.

Red velvet covers golden seats, and intricate detailing on the walls shows little of the outside. Although I'm nervous, I do know where I want to be. "How will I wave to the people of Haven from inside?" I peer back, looking to Douglas and I gesture to the saddle on Cloud.

"As you wish, Ari." He smiles, lifting me onto Clouds back. "Would you like me to ride up there with you?"

I nod my head, scared to fall off. Douglas climbs on in front of me. I look back as Willow, Aurora, and

Chloe climb into the spacious carriage with Mia.

Cloud begins to move, and people gather along the streets waving and talking to me. "You look beautiful, princess!" A young girl yells.

"Thank you!" I shout back, waving happily as we pass by.

"You okay?" Douglas asks, his voice warm.

I continue to wave, a bright smile on my face, but inside, I'm nervous. "I don't know. I haven't seen Alexander. What if—"

He doesn't let me finish his sentence. Instead he looks back to me. "He loves you; don't question or worry about that. The boy's been pacing the halls of the castle all morning in fear you were going to run."

I snort. "A nervous Alexander. I would love to see that."

"Be careful what you wish for," Douglas laughs. "He wouldn't stop talking all morning. 'What if she changed her mind? Is this wedding too much for her? Will she like it?'"

The thought warms my heart. "He should know by now that I'm here to stay."

"He does—we all do—but a man feels these things when he loves a woman." Douglas replies, looking past my shoulder longingly towards his lost love. My heart hurts for him. "I'm happy for you, Arianna. Don't ever let it go."

"I won't." I promise, my heart bursting with

emotion as the gates open upon our arrival. The castle is extravagantly decorated in an assortment of flowers and vines.

"It's gorgeous." I gasp.

One of the guard's steps forward. "Princess," he bows before helping me down. "The ceremony begins in twenty minutes. I'll bring you to your waiting quarters."

Douglas jumps off of Cloud, linking his arm through mine. "I've got her, Pendall." he tells the guard. I think he knows I'm nervous, and I appreciate the familiarity. We walk inside the castle and it shouldn't surprise me, but it's even more beautifully decorated inside.

The girls trail in behind as I take in the sights and sounds of the bustling castle. Massive vases line every inch, ones filled with blossoming flowers of all varieties. Maids and cooks clamor around, accompanied by florist checking last-minute details and adding to the ornate displays.

"Henry!" I squeal when I see him walking over to me, a cane propping most of his bodyweight. Over the past week, a few hours of each day have been dedicated to Alexander's father and his recovery. I wrap him in a hug that threatens to squeeze him into pieces.

"Princess," His eyes beam. "I mean, *Queen* Arianna. You look amazing." he tells me, looking over my dress. To our right is a photo of him and his late wife, Alexander's mother, on their wedding day. A little choked up, he brings me in for another hug.

"I'm so thankful for you coming into my boy's life."

Ruby rushes over with a smile. "Oh, Arianna! You're a sight. Come to the women's quarters!" I look towards an emotional Henry who motions for me to follow her.

We step inside the grand room and Douglas turns to stand guard outside. Willow glances at him as she passes, and I don't miss the look in her eyes as she does. Once we get settled in, I lean into her. "Why don't you just talk to him?"

"It's not that simple, and those matters are for another day. Is there anything you need?" The moment the words leave her lips she rushes out, returning a few minutes later with a bouquet. "I almost forgot! Alexander mentioned that where you're from you carry these," She grins, holding them out to me.

My heart warms at the gesture, and the fact that Alexander remembered such a small detail when I explained to him how weddings work where I come from.

"Ugh, where's the champagne?" I turn to the sound of Leah's voice, Alice in tow. Chloe crosses her arms. "What are you doing here?" she demands.

Leah takes one look at me and her dark eyes shoot daggers at my wedding gown. "If you must know, I was bringing Alex his wedding gift."

Chloe laughs. "What? A frog's leg? Troll's wart?"

"A bottle of moondust." She grins, clearly impressed with herself.

Chloe tries to hide her surprise, but she can't. I for one, have no freaking idea what they're talking about.

Alice walks over carefully. "Your dress!" she swoons.

I crouch down. "How's that ankle?"

She wiggles it a little. "It's so much better! I'm off my crutches!"

"I see that! You'll be running around in no time." I tell her.

Mia's told me stories of how close her and Alice have gotten at school. The two girls rush to the corner of the room with wide eyes to admire the ceremony site outside. I haven't looked yet, knowing that when I do it's going to make me emotional.

Leah flicks her wrist. "I would love to stay and chat, but I must leave."

"Aww, don't want to see Alexander marry his one true love?" Chloe sneers, and I almost slap my forehead.

"Hardly," She blows on her nails, dramatically. "I just have better things to do than watch Alex throw his life away to some mortal."

Chloe advances but I stop her with a raised hand. "Maybe another day, but not today." I say, smiling at Leah. With a flourish, she exits the room.

"What was that moon stuff she brought him?" I

ask curiously.

Chloe waves it off. "An extremely rare liquor. It steeps for a hundred years before they sell it, which makes it hard to find."

I throw my face in my hands. "I'm sure my stupid letter won't compare to that."

She laughs. "He's going to love your letter, and besides, you're the one he's marrying."

"True. It's just that ... she gives me weird vibes." I whisper.

Chloe rolls her eyes, agreeing with me. "All of Haven feels that way. Trust me, you're not alone."

Soft music flows in through the open windows and Willow makes her way over to me. "It's time, dear." She says.

The room clears seconds later, and I have a moment to breathe. With no one in sight, I steal a peek out of the window, watching as the chairs fill with guests. The ceremony site is breathtaking; large white flowers dot the area while floating candles illuminate everything with a romantic glow on top of daylight's already beautiful haze.

When my eyes pan to the whimsical music playing, my heart fills with joy. Mia sits with her cello, lost in her world.

"Whose idea was that?" I ask when Chloe and Aurora arrive beside me.

"Hers. Sweetest thing, right?" Chloe grins.

I nod, unable to think of words to say. "Where's Alexander?"

Aurora peeks her head around. "He should be walking up any second." But when he doesn't, a pang of nerves sits deep in my stomach.

Then, as if he knew my heart needed to see him, he walks out. Drabbed in his crisp military uniform, he heads towards the end of the aisle. Alexander stands firm, with his hands clamped in front of him, a grin from ear to ear.

"Let's get you married." Chloe giggles.

"I'll escort you to the beginning of the aisle, and the girls will take over from there." Douglas says. I take one final look back at Chloe and Aurora as they morph into their small fairy forms.

The castle doors open to the back garden, and my heart ceases in my chest. Nerves take over, the eyes of hundreds looking at me, the enormous pressure seeping in that not only am I marrying someone, I'm going to be in charge of running a country.

My pulse is running wild, until that serene moment when my eyes lock on his and Haven stands still. Finally, I calm. Alexander admires me, looking up through thick, batted lashes. His mouth is slightly agape and a wicked grin spreads across his face.

"Don't let me fall." I tell Douglas.

"I never will." he replies.

Chloe and Aurora meet us at the end of the aisle and they each grab onto my elbow.

"Woah," My feet lift off the ground, but I know they've got me. As I float down the aisle, Alexander mouths words to me. 'My bride' being one of them.

They set me down gently where he waits with an outstretched hand. "Words can't describe your beauty." he whispers, tilting his head down to meet my gaze.

I look to him, in his pressed uniform, with his styled hair. Even his one imperfection, the crescent scar on his face, is anything but imperfect.

He's stunning.

"No preacher?" I ask, looking around.

"Just us." Alexander shrugs with a soft smile.

I nod, gulping as we walk over to the three steps at the cascading overhang archway.

"Arianna Castelle, my bride," His voice is loud, powerful. "I, Alexander Hayes Thane, stand before you in the eyes of the people of Haven and the ground that the Thanes men have ruled for generations. Most importantly, I stand before you, giving you everything that I am."

I clear my throat, tears trickling down my cheeks and feeling like I'm going to pass out from both his words and the silence of hundreds of onlookers as they hang onto our every word.

"I, Arianna Itea Castelle, stand before you, a girl from another world who's desperately and uncontrollably in love with you." My gaze pans to the crowd. "I may have not been raised here, or in royalty prepped my entire life, but I promise I will always do right by Haven." The crowd smiles and I turn my attention back to Alexander. I'm proud of myself for not passing out, but something about this, about us standing before Haven, feels so right.

"I love you." he murmurs, eyes going glossy.

"I love you more than my world and yours." I say to him.

"Oh, kiss the young lad already!" Penelope yells, the crowd cheering her on. Alexander brings his face close to mine and I lean in, our lips a feather away, my heart so full of love and joy—

"Stop! Don't kiss him!" Willow shrieks.

TWENTY-FOUR

lexander studies Willow's worried face as she rushes to the altar in a frantic hurry. The crowd breaks out in hushed tones and my stomach drops.

"What are you doing?" He can't hide the anger that swirls in his eyes. Golden flakes appear, and he looks away so she doesn't see.

I catch a hint of the vines that try to creep down his cheeks and touch his face gently as he looks out to the mountain view beside us. "Alexander, breathe." I whisper with reassuring eyes.

When he calms, he looks back to us.

"Look at your fingertips, Alex." Willow tells him. Discreetly, he brings his hand to brush my cheek. The tips of his fingers, a deep purple tone.

"What's going on?" I smile nervously, trying to hide my worry.

Willow carefully places a vial in his hand. The crowd gossips louder and my nerves become almost unbearable.

"I have the kiss of death." Alexander sneers.

I lean forward to whisper. "The kiss of what?"

"He's been poisoned." Willow informs me. I refrain from gasping, instead deciding to smile to the crowd reassuringly before whispering again.

"Will he be okay?" I ask.

"I gave him an antidote." Willow gives me a solemn look. "But the poison wouldn't have hurt him; the target was you."

Alexander's fists close and he shakes with rage. "Let's just be thankful the poison gives itself away with the darkening of fingertips." Willow whispers.

"Is everything okay?" a random voice sounds from the crowd. I turn to them and notice the look of worry on everyone's face.

I fake a laugh, smiling bright. "Yes! Sorry about the theatrics." Alexander discreetly takes the vial. "This is customary in my world," I say, thankful when they believe me although they give each other odd looks. The crowd quiets and Willow takes her seat in the front row.

Guilt eats me alive for lying to them. But all other emotions melt away besides love, admiration, and forever when Alexander's strong hands grips each side of my face. He pulls me in for a kiss that's filled with such passion that it makes me lightheaded.

We pull back, grounding back to reality and turning to face the crowd with our hands interlocked.

Then, Henry stands, and the crowd goes wild from his miraculous recovery. "May I now present to you, Mr. and Mrs. Alexander Hayes Thane! Prince, and Princess of Haven." Henry presents us with a proud gleam in his eyes and an outstretched hand. Knowing our official coronation will happen later, we don't mind holding the titles of Prince and Princess for a little longer.

We bow once and head down the aisle in light, airy steps with Alexander's arm wrapped firmly around me. Once we're out of earshot, he unleashes a violent wrath upon his office, crushing a chair beneath his grip and smashing the stone wall with a single punch.

"Someone could have killed you!" he roars.

I can't wrap my head around the thought. Who would be out to get me, and why? I'm thankful for Willow always carrying around a bag filled with potions, because if not for her noticing and having the antidote for this 'kiss of death' I would die by his hand. I calm my voice to try and dull his rage. "But they didn't. Willow caught it."

He scoffs, breathing erratically. "Your life was in fucking danger, Arianna! On your wedding day!"

"It's okay, Alexander. We're okay." I tell him,

trying to calm his mind, but it's too late. He's becoming unhinged, and the moment my eyes land on his desk, I know who caused all of this.

"When I get my hands on whoever tried to murder you, by my own hand, nonetheless! I will destroy them." he seethes, vines creeping down his face.

"You don't have to look very far." I tell him.

He quirks his brow to me and I gesture to the opened bottle of moon whatever that miss sunshine gave him as a wedding gift.

"Leah." Alexander spits.

"Why would she do this?" I ask.

"Jealousy. She's vile." he grits his teeth. "She's done for. I'll kill her." he promises.

He smashes the black bottle against the wall, purple liquid and shards of glass float down.

I grit my teeth, trying to not let anger fuel my decision. "As much as I can't stand her, think of Alice."

"Your heart is too good." He slams his fist against the wooden desk, and it bows under his power until a splintered chunk flies to his feet. I shake my head when he reassures me of her demise. "Fine. I'll exile her. That's not up for discussion."

I nod, but it doesn't stop the fury inside of him. It's as if he has to purge the anger he feels, and I step back for him to do so. He rips the mantle from the wall, the roaring fire crackling below. With his hands planted on the stone, he looks up. The black vines recede as if whatever he is looking at calms him in seconds.

In curiosity, my line of sight follows his. "Is that me?" I ask, covering my heart with my hand.

"Yes." He turns. "When I was twenty, I commissioned an artist in town to draw you from my memory. It doesn't do your beauty justice, Mrs. Thane." He cracks a devilish grin.

"It was a clock." I say, looking at the oil painting that bears a striking resemblance to me.

"Mason," he growls. "Had it stuffed in a closet when he took over. I fortunately found it and placed it back where it belongs.

"You had this painted from memory?" I ask, honored.

He nods. "I've used it before battles, to ground me. Your face," His fingertips brush my cheek and butterflies fill my stomach. "Seems to be the only damn thing to bring down the animal that lives inside me."

My left hand comes up to touch his, and I notice the lack of rings we both adorn. A small laugh escapes me. "We never exchanged rings." I say.

He looks to my hand. "We didn't, did we?"

I pull his from a small pocket in my dress and slide the custom ring on his finger, earning a studious look from him.

"It's wooden. Interesting." A twinkle lays in his

eyes, much better than the fury from before.

"I went to the rubble from our cabin." I tell him, tracing the wooden ring.

"That makes it even more special." he says, planting a kiss on my forehead and pausing for a moment to steal the scent of my hair.

"We need to get back to our guests." I murmur, but there's no conviction in my tone.

"Did I tell you ..." He advances on me, pinning me against the broken desk. "How absolutely delectable you look as my wife?"

I blush. "Alexander, our guests ..." I moan.

"I just need half an hour." he promises.

"No ..." I laugh, lying.

"Okay fine! Five minutes with my bride?" he offers with a wry smile. I can't say no to that.

We stumble out of the office forty minutes later, and when we reach Douglas, Alexander gives him the order to exile Leah from Haven.

Guilt pangs in my chest for Alice, but from Alexander's and Douglas's discussion, they'll be able to visit each other. There are some things I've realized I won't be able to control, and that's why I'm thankful for the way Alexander leads, as I wouldn't be able to kick Leah out and away from her sister, but some things need to be done.

We rush downstairs to continue the celebration of

our union to find everyone drinking and dancing.

Chloe hops around me. "You're married!"

Ruby touches my cheek. "Congratulations, dear."

Willow winks. "No one thought twice of our little act. Good job, you two. Arianna, you make the most stunning bride."

Penelope claps; she's been running around all day, so I'm thankful she's taking a moment to celebrate with a glass of wine. "You really do!"

"Hey!" Mia tugs on my dress and I bend down. "Why did you lie at the ceremony?" she asks in a whisper, referring to my statement that what happened was normal where I come from.

I bite my lip, looking around to make sure no one heard her. "Mia, we're in charge of these people now. Sometimes when bad things happen, you have to keep your cool and act like nothing is wrong."

"What was bad that happened?" she pushes her brows together in confusion.

I shake my head, knowing some things are better left unsaid. "Nothing you need to worry about. Where is Alice?"

"With her parents. Her mean sister got drug out by guards earlier, and she was hiding in a closet!" Mia snickers.

"Who wants champagne?" Alexander asks, taking my mind away to celebrate.

Gerardo wheels out a silver cart filled with chilled

bottles and empty glasses. When he pops the cork and splashes of champagne sprinkle around us, I take in a deep breath of appreciation that everything went okay. Poison fears aside, there's one thing I've been waiting for.

Alfie picks up one of the small cakes, inspecting it. I reach for his wrist and lower it down. "Alfie." I whisper, unable to contain the smile that threatens to rip my face in half. "Thank you for paying your debts to Haven, but your crimes are no more and you're free to go."

"Wait," He looks between me and Alexander. "Are you serious?"

"Yes." Alexander replies with a proud grin, throwing his arm around me. "The queen developed something that will take your place as taster, and so, you're free."

His admiration, and appreciation is evident from the smile on his face. He hugs his friend Gerardo before thanking us profusely.

"It's time to celebrate." I grin, holding up a chilled glass and enjoying the night.

"That was wonderful!" I collapse onto the bed, my wedding gown feeling like it's a hundred pounds heavier after endless celebratory hours of food and dancing.

Alexander lays down beside me. "Thank you for keeping your cool at the ceremony. I hope that besides that mishap you had a fairytale wedding, as you say."

"I got flown down the aisle by fairies. I would say it was pure fairytale." I grin. "What do we do now?" I ask softly.

His fingertips graze my chin, light as a feather, and I peer up at him. "There are a few things I could think of." he says, his appetite for me insatiable. "But I've packed us up for our honeymoon."

"You remembered!" I squeal in delight.

He nods, sitting up and looking at his fingers as a checklist. "Yes, I hope I got it correctly." He appears nervous when he gazes back at me. "We take a vacation to somewhere romantic, right?"

"Exactly!" I grin, unable to contain my excitement.

Alexander sighs in relief. "Pirellia. It's a small island not far from here." He frowns, but I'm not sure why. "Sorry we can't go far from Haven, but it's a beautiful spot."

I shake my head, jumping into his lap. "Alexander, I could spend a week in this room with you and it would be perfect."

He slinks his arm around me. "That's why I love you."

"When do we leave?" I ask with a smile.

"Now," My Prince shrugs and laughs.

"This is so romantic!" I swoon, climbing into the boat.

"It was my great grandfathers; it's been in my

271

family for a long time." Alexander grins. "One day, we can pass it down to our heirs, too."

I smile thinking of our future as we set out onto the smooth water. Luminescent mushrooms cast an ambient light in the forest far away as the waves gently rock our little boat. Stars illuminate stunning, dark blue water beneath our quaint little ride. My eyes spot a few colorful aquatic creatures, each more magical than the last, as they dance around our boat beneath the waves. Within the nearby forest, I can hear birds and wolves singing their nightly songs. Beautiful doesn't even begin to describe it.

"The night sky is so clear." I lean back to get a better view, but I don't miss Alexander's gaze on me.

As we near the island, I can faintly make out the shape of what looks to be a modern-style house. Much more modern than anything I've seen in Haven, anyway.

I gasp when the entirety of the massive structure comes into view.

Dark wooden beams encase pristine white walls, ones that shine faintly like pearls underneath the moonlight guiding us to the lone dock that sits at the edge of the island. Impossibly long windows wrap around the rectangular house, and a few luxurious lounge chairs beneath hanging trees greet us after we step off our boat, luggage in tow.

Sand slips into my shoes and I grimace, but it's easy to ignore when the beauty of this romantic gesture takes over my senses completely.

While we're only about a ten-minute journey from the castle, it's private and romantic. "Look! You can see Haven in the distance!" I gesture out, seeing the tops of houses and speckles of lights.

"I love that you're going to stand beside me while I lead my land." Alexander muses. I tilt my head, squinting my eyes at him. "Our land." he corrects himself.

"Always," I respond, yawning. The events of the day are getting to me. Suddenly, I realize I've forgotten something important. "Shit!"

"What?" he asks, concern filling his features.

"Nothing," I reply sheepishly. He sends me a funny look and I break my resolve, throwing my hands up. "Willow gave me something, and I forgot it." I left behind my entire bag, including my dream potion.

"What something?" He can't hold back his grin.

I blanket my blush with my hair. "For our wedding night, she told me," I look at him. "For us to take ..."

"Oh, I see." He winks. "We don't need any magic or potions for that. Have you seen yourself?"

I flush crimson when he sweeps in for a heated kiss, only letting go so he can lead us towards our getaway.

Glass floor-to-ceiling windows give a clear look into the condo. It's dimly lit by a faint, golden glow from hundreds of candle flames that dance inside.

The scent of roses beckons us to the front door,

and Alexander smirks, looking me up and down.

"I guess now I'll be carrying you," he chuckles, setting down our bags.

"What-" I begin before being cut off as he swoops me into his arms. "Alexander!"

He laughs outright. My Prince, my husband, my soulmate. If anything, that laugh makes this experience all the more perfect. "What? It's a tradition for honeymoons, right?"

Soft, gentle music sweeps through the space.

"The girls came here before we left and got it ready for us." he says, his tone deep and earthy. We walk towards the bedroom with me still laying in his arms, not allowing our gazes to trail from one another.

"Is it safe here? Did they ..." I ask, looking around the bedroom with butterflies in my stomach.

"Yes, the house is enchanted. We can have all the fun we want tonight." Alexander grins.

He sets me down and begins to unbutton my dress painfully slow, taking his time to pepper kisses along my skin as it becomes exposed. "Hurry, husband." I beg, craving him.

"I'm taking my time with your body tonight." he replies in a heady tone, eyes raking over my exposed skin with desire and so much more.

We spend the night in blissful serenity together, completely tangled in body and soul.

As morning came, I had reached for him but felt the pang of his absence in the bed. "Alexander!" I called out, sure that he was awake and working on plans for Haven. I waited for the rustle of his feet to sound, but I heard nothing except the soothing sounds of the tide rolling outside our bedroom window.

I opened my eyes to get up, and darkness enveloped me. Hauntingly black nothingness surrounding me at every corner.

"Alexander!" I screamed then, fear coursing through every bone as I stood up, my feet hitting the black ground. I began to run as fast as I could through the endless pit.

"Ari, baby. You're having a nightmare again. Wake up." a soothing voice told me. I could hear him faintly, but I couldn't escape the heavy darkness that was slowly pulling me under.

The sensation went from falling into nothingness to being engulfed and trapped by darkness.

My wrists were pinned, and I struggled with every ounce of energy I had. "Help me!" I pleaded, desperate when I saw his face in the darkness.

Only without the crescent shaped scar. "Hey there, beautiful." Mason's putrid tone leaked into my ears. He lunged for me, but instead of cowering or running, I felt an unexplainable surge of power course through me, and with every ounce of energy I had, I lifted my hands to defend myself.

A gleaming light leaked through my palms, and then it shot out.

My eyes fly open, awakening from a terrifying dream and escaping from my worst nightmare.

"Ari!" Alexander flies through the room, crashing through thick glass and landing outside. I rush after him, trembling.

"I was dreaming, I thought you were Mason!" I cry out, staring at my hands and cursing them for what they had just done.

My knees dig into the hot sand, attempting to shake him awake but he doesn't budge. "Alexander, please get up!" I beg.

My eyes roam the little island for any sign of help, any sign of life. Realizing just how small it is in the dawn of morning, I begin to lose hope. What have I done?

I rush inside the condo, hastily trying to figure out how I'm going to carry this massive man.

I gasp slightly in relief when I find the keys to the boat. Rushing to his side again, I kiss his forehead, hoping by now he has healed and woken up but he's still, and the warmth is leaving his body.

"Why aren't you waking up?" I scream.

Burying my face in my hands, tears stream down

my cheeks. I don't understand what's happened. Why when I tried to stop Mason in my dream, that Alexander got thrown back in my reality.

The boat is wading against the small current, and its mechanical system is unfamiliar to me. I slam my fist against the wheel and scream the only thing I know can save us. "Cloud!"

Back by Alexander's side, I look to the sky. My racing pulse slows when I see glorious white wings flowing through the clouds.

"You are such a good boy!" I tell him with a fierce promise of all the carrots in the world when he lands on the sand beside us.

He's majestic, with his massive wings at full span at his incredible stance. I'm mesmerized by the beauty. It's something to take my mind off my aching heart when my arms travel between Alexander's back and the warm sand.

With strength I never knew that I had, I lift his massive body from the ground and place him on Cloud's back. I climb on, holding onto my world with my trembling hands. "Bring me to Willow, Cloud. Hurry!"

I hold on tight to Alexander as we ascend into the sky. I don't have time to think about the experience I'm going through on his back, and I'm thankful when the morning streets are vacant when we arrive at Willow's shop.

She rushes outside, her eyes widening when she

sees Alexander laid out, lifeless in front of me. "What's wrong? What happened?" she cries.

With a panged tone in my voice and tears spilling from my cheeks, I speak. "I think ... I think I killed him."

TWENTY-FIVE

"Come inside darling, help me carry him." Willow says. She's trying to stay calm, but she's having a hard time controlling her rapid breathing.

As we slide his body onto the table, Willow shoves everything off of it. Glass bottles and vials break at our feet. I lock the doors, shutting the curtains to give us privacy.

"What happened?" She rustles around, grabbing random things.

"I hurt him, Willow." I can barely speak; all I do is hold his limp hand.

"I'm making you some tea. You look frightened." she says.

I burst into tears and they fall like droplets to the ground. "He's supposed to wake up!" She hands me the cup of tea while we stand over Alexander's lifeless body. "Do something." I plead.

"Tell me everything." Willow normally has a way of making me feel comforted, and I know she's trying, but I can't bear the sight in front of me.

I rush through, waving my hands in a frantic way. "We were at the island and I had a nightmare."

"What about your dream tonic?" she inquires.

"I've been taking it! But I forgot to bring it last night. Alexander packed everything and ... oh my god. What did I do?" I bellow.

"Breathe, Arianna," she reasons with me, speaking in a calm voice. "Tell me what happened."

I take a few deep breaths and sip on the warm tea she's handed me, but nothing works to ease the utter despair in my heart.

"I had a nightmare, and this like bright light shot from my hands! But it really happened in real life! Alexander took the brunt of whatever force came from me." I cry out, holding my palms flush to showcase.

"I knew this would happen." she mutters, the back of her hand caressing Alexander's cheek.

I shake my head. "You knew what would happen?" I dare to ask, confused by the knowing tone in her voice.

Willow gestures to the chair beside us. "You may want to take a seat." she suggests, but I decline, unable to sit or do anything besides hold Alexander's hand.

"Why?" I ask, confused about the stillness of everything. We need to be moving, figuring out a solution, not chatting.

"Arianna." She sits down herself. "Do you ever wonder why your middle name is Itea?"

"My mother gave it to me." I respond, not sure why this conversation is taking place.

She shakes her head, watching me intently. "Honey, I gave you that name."

My head rolls back in frustration. "No. What are you talking about? My mother did!"

"I did, darling. Itea is a variation of Willow. You're my daughter." she says, unflinching.

"You're lying!" I scream back.

She pulls a vial full of truth serum from under her desk and chugs it. My hands tremble as she speaks. "You're my daughter." she repeats.

"It can't be ... my mom—"

Willow raises a hand to stop me. "She is your mother in every right. She raised you when I couldn't bear to risk your life here in Haven."

"I come from here?" I stammer.

She nods. "Did you ever wonder why there are no baby pictures of you? When you were a toddler, even?"

I shrug my shoulders, my body feeling like it's going into shock. "My father was abusive. I always assumed he threw them away. That's what she told me when we left."

She cringes. "That vile creature who Alexander told me about is not your father."

"Then who is?" I demand, but I already know the answer by the way she looks away. "It's Douglas, isn't it?" I exclaim in disbelief.

"Yes, but ..."

"He doesn't know?"

"No, he does. That's why he looks at you that way. That's why he watches Mia and the reason he wanted to walk you down the aisle." she admits sheepishly.

"So, everyone's been lying to me?" My words are slow, and my mind is reeling. None of this matters right now. Alexander is hurt.

She shakes her head, frown lines prominent. "Only me, Douglas, and my best friend ever knew. The woman who raised you, Marisett."

Hearing her say my mother's name makes me still. "Why didn't you come with me? Why didn't you want me?" I feel like I'm going to throw up.

"Darling, my heart has been shattered since the moment I sent you through the portal, but I couldn't protect you here, and I'm not a strong enough witch to travel through lands like she was."

"Protect me from what?" I ask.

Willow looks down to Alexander's still body. "From him," she whispers into the still air.

I scoff, not believing a word she says. "He would never hurt me."

"It's in your fate and it is sealed, my sweet girl. You and Alexander are destined to destroy each other. This is what I was protecting you from."

"Our love is good!" I cry.

She nods. "And the world is cruel, Arianna. For two pure soulmates like you to be together? That love is catastrophic, too large to live in one world. We had no choice but to separate you two"

"I don't believe you." Tears trickle down my cheeks and a sob rips itself from my throat. "Just help him!" I beg.

"He'll be fine, dear. It's the first shockwave of your power unleashing. If you weren't dulled by the potion you've been taking, things would be much worse." She tilts her head, looking into my eyes. "He'll wake up dear ... this time."

"This time? Are you threatening him?" Her sincere tone makes me think not, but what kind of statement is that?

A small smile breaks through her teared cheeks. "No! I love you both too much to risk something happening to you."

I shake my head in disbelief. "None of this makes sense! I have powers but they're dulled? It's insane!"

"The potion I gave you suppresses your powers."

she tells me. I almost question her more until I look to the empty vial of truth serum in her hands. I know first-hand that it doesn't allow you to lie.

"You can't lie." I whisper. "What about Mia? She's not my sister?" Tears soak my cheeks.

"Not by blood, but by every way that matters, she is."

"How did I come back?" I stammer.

"You were both so determined, feeling out of place, and your hearts brought you home. It's what allowed you to break through the barrier. I assumed the potion would be enough for some time while I tried to figure out our next steps."

I stare down at the man who is invincible, realizing I'm the only thing that can hurt him. "What do I do to protect him?"

"To protect him, and you, you'll have to return to your home." She frowns, tears welling heavy in her eyes.

"This *is* my home!" I cry.

She rushes to my side, wrapping me in a tight hug. "I love you so much, my sweet girl. This will always be your home. But you have to go."

"There has to be another way ... he heals." I plead.

"He doesn't heal from you, Ari. When the darkness took him—"

"You knew?" I interrupt, shocked.

"Of course. It radiates from him." She sighs. "He

was a rowdy boy who turned into a warrior when he became a man. I noticed the changes, and also his inability to tell anyone about the darkness. But I knew when he would heal, as he was only coming to me for help." She dabs a tear from her cheek. "When the darkness took over him, every scar, every bone, they all healed. I knew when it happened, and I took comfort in him being invincible. But every morning, I would see the pain he was in. Sometimes he would let it heal on his own, or he would come see me."

I gasp, realizing our dreams hurt him. He never let me know to protect me. "He always heals." Is all I can say.

The tip of her finger traces along the crescent scar on his face. "Except for the cut you gave him as a child."

"I did that?" I ask and struggle not to pass out when she nods.

Willow carefully walks over to a safe and opens it, revealing a stack of albums. She flips to a page, and the sound that emanates in her chest as she looks at it almost breaks me. "Here," She sniffles, handing it to me.

I look down, watching the video on paper as I sit by a lake on a blanket. It's a glowing summer day, and I'm maybe three years old. Alexander walks over, about five, and sits beside me. I look up from the photo for a second to find my newfound mother crying.

As I look back down, I watch a young Willow walk up and kiss my cheek. A loving mother who fixes her child's hair and prepares a cheeseboard on the blanket.

There's no sound in this magical photo, only silence. But I can imagine the way I'm giggling when I throw my head back, my red hair flowing in the breeze.

Alexander's mother, who I recognize from photos at the castle, walks up from the water, a younger Henry beside her. The camera turns, and my mother smiles at the lens. I've never seen a video of her so young.

When it pans back to us, I'm happily munching on some sort of meat. A moment passes and I grip the handle of the knife, not understanding what it is at such a young age. I throw my hand back when Willow tries to grab it from me, in turn slicing Alexander's face open.

He touches his cheek but doesn't cry. When little me sees the blood, I do. His mom, the queen, holds a napkin to it. Willow then hovers her hand over his face, healing him. He hugs me when I refuse to stop crying and the parents smile as they watch us.

So many secrets between them, hidden away in a safe for no one to remember.

I slam the book shut, refusing to believe this. "This is too much, there has to be another way."

"You'll always find him, and you'll always find each other. You have to return." Willow sighs.

I shake my head. "He'll dream of me again."

"I've created his own tonic. While yours suppresses your powers, it also halts your dreams. His will stop his dreams entirely, as well, but he will keep his strength. I will administer it to him daily."

I cry out, reaching for the vial and wanting to smash it against the wall. "Don't. We can figure this out."

"I knew you would try, and I commend you for that, but it's too risky." she says, holding the vial out of my reach.

Tears burn my cheeks. "When he wakes up, I'll tell him, and we will make the decision together."

Willow looks remorseful, her head hanging low. "None of that will matter, darling. You won't remember anything that happened this morning."

She gestures to the cup of tea on the counter and I gasp from the realization. Walking over to it, I sprinkle some of our powder, checking for poison. "I wouldn't harm you dear. I needed to make you forget." she stammers, her lip trembling.

I take the cup and smash it on the ground. Shards of ceramic shatter at my feet. "He won't forget me. It doesn't matter what you do." I sneer.

Her heart breaks before me and tears begin to fall down her face. "I'm sending you back through the portal. Anyone here who isn't tied to you by blood will forget just like last time." Willow says, now sobbing uncontrollably. The harsh betrayal eating her.

"There's no way I could have forgotten any of you." I tell her.

"We pulled your memories. Wiped them away.

You were so young it's hard to imagine you would have remembered, but that didn't make it any easier on me or your father."

"Willow, please." I beg. "What about Mia? Will she forget me?"

"No, you're going together." Willow croaks, wiping her face with her sleeve and attempting to contain herself. "I love you so much, Itea." she whispers. With one final fleeting spout of energy, I hurl myself over Alexander's body before I black out.

TWENTY-SIX

I rub my eyes, stretching my sore muscles. "So, he'll be okay?" I look to Willow, confused.

"Yes, dear. He's going to be just fine." she assures me with a smile that doesn't reach her eyes. Tears stain her cheeks.

"Why are you crying so much then?" I ask, looking around the dark shop with the curtains drawn.

"You two just scared me, that's all." She appears broken and lost.

Chloe frantically rushes in. "Oh, thank Haven you're here!"

"What's wrong?" My tone is pained from the panic in her tone.

"Oh my god!" She points to Alexander. "What happened to him?"

"Umm, I don't ..." I rack my brain trying to remember. "I don't really know."

"He fell. You know how he's always getting hurt. He'll be up soon." Willow reassures us. I try to recall how long I've been at Willow's shop or how I got here, but all I can focus on is that Alexander's been hurt.

But the words keep repeating in my head that he's okay. I can go. "He'll wake up soon. What's going on?" I ask, my mind free of fear or worry about Alexander. I know he's going to be okay.

"Mia was missing, but she's here somewhere." Chloe's sense of urgency seems to deplete.

"I haven't seen her!" I state, but she doesn't look too worried.

Chloe shrugs, looking around. "She's around here somewhere, we can look around." she suggests.

"Can you stay with him?" I ask Willow.

She nods, dabbing under her cheeks with a napkin. "Of course, dear." Willow replies, her eyes glistening. "And Ari, when you find her, both of you meet me by the mushroom forest okay? I have a really wonderful recipe for a healing potion that I want to show you. I figured Mia would be interested too considering how well she's doing in that class."

"Yeah, as soon as we find her." I say. I swoop down to give Alexander a kiss. My cheeks are soaked but I'm assuming my lack of remembrance and the way my hands are shaking is because of shock from seeing him fall.

Me and Chloe head out of the shop, and I look to her. "Weren't you watching her last night?"

She nods, her eyes roaming around the empty street. "Yeah, but I'm not worried anymore. She's probably with Douglas or something."

"You were just freaking out." I state.

"Yeah, but a few people told me Alexander came by and they thought she went with him, but I thought you two were still at the island." She winks, nudging me. "I looked around for a while, but now that I know you're here, she's got to be around here somewhere." She shrugs.

I stop in my tracks, and through the fog in my brain one thing I do know with certainty is that we never saw Mia today. "Chloe, Alexander never came by." My stomach drops, realization flooding me. "Mason's alive."

We both look to each other, and then run as fast as we can, seemingly going nowhere. "What happened this morning?" Chloe gasps, her pink hair flowing behind her.

I look away, trying to recall the memory but its distant. "I don't know, Chloe. I can't remember anything!"

"Did you two get wasted last night?" she asks, raising a brow.

I begin to hyperventilate, shaking my head. "How will we find her? What if he hurts her?" I don't know what he's capable of, and that terrifies me.

She stops, looking around and taking my hand to

guide me. "He won't hurt her. He wants something, and we're going to find her."

"How?"

We approach an unfamiliar forest and step inside. Day becomes night and a familiar blackness surrounds us. "It's so dark." I say.

"Keep quiet, only whisper." she warns.

We trudge through the forest, my eyes adjusting slightly. "Where are we going?"

"The only place in Haven surrounded by dark magic." She gulps. "We're going where the lost things go." I swallow down my fears and push forward in silence, sinking deeper into the wretched darkness. "A few more minutes." she tells me.

A deep chill creeps up my spine when we get to a lake; evil lives here. "Why is the water black?"

She huffs in disgust. "It's tainted, but it's the only way we can find her."

"How does it work?" I ask, looking down.

She pulls a single hair from her pocket. "This is from Mia's cello string. If I couldn't find you guys, I was planning on coming here alone." She tiptoes to the edge of the water and drops the hair into the abyss.

We both tilt our heads over the water, and an image shows on the surface. I see Mia, sitting by a fire. A hauntingly familiar scene. "Did you guys rebuild the cabin?" I gasp.

"We started. It's not completely done, but that's exactly where they are."

I lose my balance, knowing that she's with Mason where magic can't go. I'm frantic, pacing the edge of the black water, but when my right foot barely touches the surface, memories rush through me.

"I'm a witch." I state, in a trance.

"What?" Chloe croaks, and we both pay attention to the black surface in front of us.

Vivid insights of my lost memories surface on the black water. Willow holding me on a stormy night. Douglas giving me piggyback rides. Playing with Alexander at the castle. Birthdays, the final one being my third before the last slide plays before me. The sorrowful sight of Willow's face as she hands me over, into the arms of the woman who raised me, in the mushroom forest.

Me and Chloe don't say anything; we've both understood what happened. I stepped into where the lost things go, and now I'm not lost anymore.

"We have to go back to get Willow." I state, putting on a brave face. "And to see if Alexander's woken up."

Chloe thinks for a moment. "We can teleport."

I shake my head. "Why didn't we before? Let's go!"

"This place is dark, and it was too risky that we would get separated. But with two of us, and you being a witch," A smirk plays on her face. "Give me your hands." she says.

"Okay," I play along, gripping firmly onto her open palms.

"Now think of the shop, think of Willow, and close your eyes."

"We're here." I breathe in relief until my eyes pan to the table where Alexander once was. Now, his body is replaced by a note.

"'Meet me where our dreams were burned.' It says, and shivers rake through me.

"Hmph!" a muffled sound captures our attention.

We investigate, walking through the shop towards the muffled screams until we open the closet door. Willow is tied, the rope seemingly burning her skin.

"What happened?" I demand, carefully taking off her restraints so she can speak.

She looks between us, unsure. "Umm,"

"We went where the lost things go." Chloe tells her and Willow perks up, apologizing.

"Arianna, I'm so sorry. I never meant to—"

I cut her off with a gentle wave. We can talk about this after we find him. "What happened?" Chloe asks.

"Mason." Willow cries out. "He came in, and Alexander got up and just followed him. I don't know where he went!"

"I have an idea," I say, holding up the note. Willow reads it, understanding.

"We're teleporting." Chloe says, holding her hands out.

"I'll catch up." Willow says.

I tilt my head, looking over her. "Don't be afraid to use your magic. We need you."

She hesitates, but we can't waste any time. I grip Chloe's hands and teleport with her to the edge of the enchanted forest.

"Take down the barrier." I order gently.

She claps her hands. "Done."

In moments, we stand at the cabin, but I know Mason's tricks and I don't want to risk rushing inside like last time.

"Arianna, don't come any closer!" Alexander comes from the side. His eyes gleam golden. Dark vines no longer slowly creep down his eyes, they're set on his face now, twining around his crescent scar and suffocating his sharp features.

He's fighting within himself, with his darkness.

"Where's Mia?" I cry out.

He nudges his head. "She's inside. I can't ... I can't control it. I can't protect you."

"Come here!" Chloe begs him.

Before any more is said, the front door bursts open and Mason steps out. "Oh, what a nice surprise this is," The sound of his laughter makes bile rise in my throat.

"Mason, if you hurt her—" I threaten before he

cuts me off.

"Oh, I won't be the one to hurt her." He smiles, pointing to Alexander. "He will."

"He won't touch her." I sneer.

Alexander shakes his head. "Ari, I can't."

"Fight it!" I demand, my body feeling like it's on fire.

Blackness oozes around Alexander, swirling like smoke. Mason takes a step down the stairs. "You see, my dear, much like how you two are soulmates, or whatever-"

Chloe cuts him off, stomping her small foot into the dirt. "Why aren't you dead already?" she growls.

Mason flicks his wrist again. "Get rid of her, brother." he tells Alexander.

With the swoop of Alexander's hand, Chloe is thrown hard, her back crashing into a nearby tree. I scream, but I'm rooted where I stand, unable to turn towards the monster that is controlling my husband.

Mason continues his tyrannical speech. "I was so jealous of his darkness. What a gift that he just puts to waste!" His maniacal laugh booms through the forest. "Then I realized I could use him as my puppet." He claps his hands, amused by himself.

He admires Chloe who is passed out by the trunk of the tree before speaking again.

"As I was saying, before the fairy rudely interrupted me, Alex and I share a very special bond like you and him do."

Mason takes a step closer to me, and Alexander emits a sound from deep within his chest, but there's nothing he can do.

"Just leave him alone!" I cry out.

Mason shakes his head. "As long as he lives with darkness inside of him, I come back to life every time he helplessly tries to kill me. Because I am the true darkness of our bloodline; I live for the dark. The darkness was mine!" he roars, then laughs. "But I guess now, it's mine again."

"How are you controlling him?" I ask, trying to devise a plan to save the one I love.

Leah walks up from inside the cabin, crossing her arms and showing me a sinister smile. "He had help with tying his bond to make them one." She sneers. "In case you didn't catch that, it's me. I'm the one who helped him after Alex decided to kick me out of Haven."

"I don't understand." I say. How could she do this? Doesn't she care for him at all? No, it was about the crown for her and with Mason, she has power. They're perfect together.

"Did you not hear a word I just said to you?" Mason chides, rolling his eyes.

"You're a coward!" I scream at him.

He shakes his head, waving a finger at me.

"No, he is." he scoffs. "I had plans to kill you both.

It was so perfect creeping into your dreams this morning." He laughs, and I try to hide the tremble of fear in my hands. "A tiny island surrounded by water! What a fucking idiot for him placing you there, but then that damn unicorn showed up before he died." He waves it off. "Oh well. It all worked out in my favor in the long run." He turns his attention to Alexander. "Squeeze the life from your bride's neck, brother." Mason hisses.

I submit when Alexander advances on me, knowing this is the one thing I will never fight. Knowing that I'll never harm him, even if it kills me.

But Mia.

Mason struts back inside with Leah dangling on his arm and from the crack in the door I see Mia sitting by the fire, unharmed. I have no choice but to fight for her.

Alexander walks slowly, fighting against the instincts he's having. "Please run, baby."

"No, Alexander. We can get through this. We can get through anything." I promise him.

His feet land in front of me, and a sinister smile rises on his lips. "Not this." Alexander sneers, the evil taking over.

His hands grip my throat, and within seconds I feel myself going faint.

Then, a powerful urge takes over me. One that I can't explain. I place my hands on his shoulders as he sucks the life from me.

I begin to do the same but pulling the darkness from him. "Ale ..." I begin, but I can't speak. His grip is too strong. But the more the darkness invades me, the stronger I feel, and the weaker his grip becomes.

Finally, he lets go.

"Ari." He coughs, gripping me for a hug. His golden speckled eyes return to blue, and the rose like vines on his face recede, but he looks terrified for me.

"Are you okay?" I ask him, touching his face

"Me? Are you okay?" He looks confused. "I don't have a desire to destroy you anymore." he says, touching a piece of my hair. I look at it in his hands to find the strand is no longer crimson but instead jet black. "What's happening?" Alexander asks.

"Long story, but I'm a witch, and we were friends when I was little." He looks at me dumbfounded, and I smile. "We have to save Mia now." Willow appears beside me out of thin air. "You used your magic." I sigh in relief, thankful to have more help and feeling indestructible.

"Of course. I couldn't let my only daughter be alone." She touches my hair, frowning. "You siphoned his darkness."

"Daughter?" Alexander exclaims, utterly confused.

"Long story." Willow replies. "Where's Mia?"

A door flies open, and Mason walks out. "Is that beautiful wife of yours dea—" His eyes pan from me, to Alexander, to Willow, and the most beautiful look of terror washes over his face.

I step towards him, without fear. "Nope, not dead. I'm stronger now. I can feel it in my veins." I laugh, darkness now at my fingertips. "And guess what Mason? I'm not your blood, so you can't control me."

Mason attempts to retreat inside but I won't allow it. I take away his free will to walk by lifting my hand. He goes with it, hovering over the air, suspended by my grip. A violent breeze rattles the trees, reminding me of mine and Alexander's dreams.

I bring Leah with him, hovering her body near his. She's an evil sidekick in this story, and nothing more than a safe harbor of evil for Mason to land. They both deserve to be destroyed.

Willow's voice is distant and muffled but I can decipher her words through the whooshes of wind. "Be careful, dear. Alex's darkness has turned into black magic for you. The power can be addicting." she warns.

I don't listen. I continue to lift Mason high above me, the bright light that beamed from my palms earlier now a deep, obsidian shade as it shoots from my hands and wraps around Mason's floating body.

His desperate cries do nothing to stop me.

"Arianna. Please, darling, don't let it consume you." Willow pleads.

Little does she know that I can feel it draining from my fingertips. I scream as I expel the evil from my palms until the black turns back to white and a bright light turns Mason and Leah into a sparkling pile of ash overhead, the remnants floating down around us, showering the forest.

"Woah! Cool!" Mia claps, and I'm broken from my trance.

"Mia!" I cry, rushing to her side and pulling her in for a hug. "You're okay." I gasp.

"Yeah! Alexander brought me here and I sat by the fire watching this really cool thing. It's like a TV but not." she rambles, and I've never been so happy to hear her gibberish. "Anyways, everyone wouldn't stop yelling so I came outside, and you did like a firework show!"

She's unfazed and completely unaware of what just occurred and I'm so thankful. "Did you see anything else?" I ask.

"You can do magic!" she squeals.

I grin, nearly collapsing in relief on the stairs to the cabin. I'm thankful her mind doesn't have to endure the trauma of seeing her big sister making a man and woman turn to ash.

Mia tilts her head, studying me. "Your hair's changing colors."

I touch my strands, watching before my eyes as they flow back to crimson. But a black streak remains, framing my face

Alexander pulls me into a hug from behind, whipping me around to face him. "You foolish, beautiful girl." he tells me, nearly toppling over from exhaustion as he grips the railing.

My lips dive into his and they don't leave until Chloe limps towards us, confused and in pain.

I rush to her, checking over her body. A wide bruise lays on her back, the result of her small body slamming into the hard wood of the tree.

"I'm fine." She assures me with a smile, but she allows me to help her walk. "What did I miss?" she asks.

Alexander runs his hand across my back. "Just Ari being a total badass!"

"Bad word!" Mia shouts.

"Sorry, Mia." he replies. We all chuckle, catching our breath from the moment we experienced.

"I'll clear the cabin." Alexander states, walking Mia up to let her watch more movies while we de-stress.

Willow stands far away from us, unsure in her stance.

I help Chloe to the step so she can sit. Turning, I walk up to Willow and wrap my arms around her neck. "I'm so sorry I was overwhelmed earlier. I can't imagine how hard this has been for you. Seeing me, but never being able to say anything."

She bursts into tears, holding me against her. "It's not your fault, sweetie! I'm just so happy both of you are okay.

I whisper so only she can hear. "Do you think we

can stay? Am I still a danger to him?"

Willow gives me one regretful shake of her head, but Chloe charges forward with a painful grunt. "You're not going anywhere!" she orders.

"How did you hear that?" I ask, looking around.

She points to her pink hair. "Super awesome fairy ears, duh!"

Willow frowns. "They have no choice. It's to keep them safe. Believe me, I would do anything to keep Arianna here with us, but her safety is more important than breathing for me." She replies, walking around to look at the source of Chloe's pain. She hands her a vile from something in her pocket, and Chloe gulps it down with a scrunched, angry face.

Alexander returns, looking pissed. "My wife isn't going anywhere. What is going on?" he demands.

I turn to Willow. "Give his memories back to him. I know that you can." I clear my throat, looking at the others. "I'm not mad, but we're adults now, and we can make these decisions on our own."

Alexander's brow furrows in frustration. "What memories are you talking about?"

Willow retrieves a glass vial filled with black liquid. She touches the obsidian water with her fingertip and presses it to his forehead. Everything flows through him. His eyes open wide, and a far off look takes over his face as the memories he was too young to remember and ones that were stolen replay in his mind.

"That explains ... so much." he finally says.

Willow nods her head. "So now you can see why one world can't contain the two of you."

"There has to be another way." he thinks aloud, pacing the area.

Chloe throws her hands up in frustration.

"Hello! I've been trying to speak for like ages over here." We all turn our attention to her, and she huffs, blowing a strand of pink away from her face, "As I was trying to say, they aren't a threat to each other anymore. With the darkness leaving Alexander—" Chloe begins before being cut off by Willow.

"The darkness inside Alexander came later. That was never the problem when I had to send her away. The evil that invaded him was just a sliver of what they would have to endure in one world. It was merely a cosmic force of them trying to be together through their dreams."

Chloe agrees. "I know but hear me out. Black magic, darkness, it always comes with a price."

Willow shakes her head. "Chloe," she warns. "That's never what I wanted for her."

"Think, Willow." Chloe urges.

And she does, and a smile creeps upon her face, followed by tears. Happy tears.

"It's not her soul, it's mine." Alexander states.

I throw my palm on my forehead. "I'm so

confused."

Alexander grabs my hands. "You gained a part of my soul when you extracted the darkness from me. You saved us."

"Will you be hurt now?" I ask.

Alexander brings his face to mine, and for a few blissful moments, we inhale the fresh air around us. Serenity. "Not at all, and since you have part of my soul, no cosmic force can get in the way of us being together."

Willow beams with joy. "You're intertwined now. It would be more dangerous for both of you if you left."

Everyone steps away to give me a moment with Willow. From the forest, Douglas emerges with his head hanging low.

"Arianna," He breathes the biggest sigh of relief, his eyes glossed over. "You're okay."

"And you're my father." I smile when he looks like he's on the verge of collapsing.

Willow lets her tears flow freely now. "I'm so sorry we sent you away. I was only trying to protect you. It destroyed us."

"Don't, please. Don't apologize. If we never went to my world, Mia would never have been born." I look back to see her playing tag with Alexander, and I know that now is how it was always meant to be.

"Do you forgive me?" she asks, and Douglas places his hands on her shoulders in a sense of unity.

"Do you forgive us?" he adds, conviction seeping through his tone. They gave their only daughter up to keep her safe, and it ruined them both. I saw them in the old video, the love they held for each other and still do.

"There's nothing to forgive. You were protecting a child you love." I tell them, tears trickling down each of our cheeks.

Willow pulls me in for a hug and Douglas wraps his arms around both of us.

Everything feels perfectly in place.

I'm home.

ONE YEAR LATER

My world has quite literally changed. But one constant has always remained, Alexander.

My love for him has grown to deeper lengths with every passing day.

My reality now is so much better than my dreams.

Mia is thriving here, in her studies and her music. Most importantly, she's happy.

Willow has brought new warmth to my heart. I see her daily, along with her husband-again, my father, Douglas.

And with one year of leading Haven under my belt, I've discovered that I was meant for this. To help and rule beside Alexander.

During our coronation, when Henry placed the golden crown on my head, I knew in that moment, this was what I was meant to do.

Alexander's grown so much, taking over his father's duties and doing it with unwavering grace.

There are so many things to be grateful for in our lives but right now, the baby in my belly is giving us an extra special reason to celebrate.

Laying on a fluffy rug inside our cabin, with our legs intertwined and a roaring fire warming our toes, we take in the quiet moment together.

Alexander caresses my face. "I love you, Arianna Itea Thane." His lips press onto my forehead for a lingering, precious moment.

I trace the crescent moon, winding my fingertip along his scar and to his chiseled jaw. My heart pounds every time he looks at me. "And I love you, more than this world and mine, Alexander Hayes Thane. You're my Haven in a storm." I tell him breathlessly.

AND THEY LIVED

happily

EVER AFTER…

ACKNOWLEDGMENTS

Sending out a huge THANK YOU to everyone who made publishing Haven possible.

My husband, who supports me in every dream. Love is whenever I'm with you. Also, Luna loves me more.

My editor, Ashley Oliver. ~~Your~~… ~~Youre~~… You're awesome! Thank you for all of your help! And y'all, not only is she an editor, but also an author!

My cover designer, Jessica Scott. A constant in every one of my book acknowledgements. I am so thankful for you!

My family, caffeine, I'm starting to feel like I'm writing an acceptance speech for an award… haha.

THANK YOU!